SUMMER IN FRANCE

SUMMER IN FRANCE

Vanessa Graham

This Large Print book is published by BBC Audiobooks Ltd, Bath, England and by Thorndike Press®, Waterville, Maine, USA.

Published in 2004 in the U.K. by arrangement with the author.

Published in 2004 in the U.S. by arrangement with Juliet Burton Literary Agency.

U.K. Hardcover   ISBN 1–4056–3067–1(Chivers Large Print)
U.K. Softcover   ISBN 1–4056–3068–X(Camden Large Print)
U.S. Softcover   ISBN 0–7862–6845–X (Nightingale)

The text of this Large Print edition is unabridged.
Other aspects of the book may vary from the original edition.

Set in 16 pt. New Times Roman.

Printed in Great Britain on acid-free paper.

British Library Cataloguing in Publication Data available

Library of Congress Control Number: 2004107513

CHAPTER ONE

Immediately below the window the white paving of the terrace shimmered blindingly in the Mediterranean sun, edged by massed banks of mimosa and early roses. Beyond them lay a stretch of garden and then the sea itself, picture-postcard blue and dotted with gently rocking pleasure boats.

Caroline surprised in herself a bubble of sheer happiness—the first she had felt for six months—and resolutely brushed away the underlying guilt. Mourning for her father had to stop some time, and the proposed two-month stay at the Villa Mimosa seemed an ideal chance to reassess her position.

True, she had been forced to leave college before the final exams, and the academic career she had planned was now closed to her. But on the credit side, that secretarial course she had embarked on so casually one vacation had proved an unexpected asset, and she was incredibly lucky to have found a position as secretary to the famous novelist Adeline Stevens—even without the bonus of two months' work in the South of France.

It was time to put the past behind her and take a more active part in living again. And one of the first priorities must be a regained interest in her appearance. She turned from

1

the window to lean over the dressing-table and examined her reflection critically. The girl who looked apprehensively back at her was very different from the pretty, bubbling self of seven months ago. The large, amber-coloured eyes were ringed with shadows, the fine skin too tightly drawn over high cheekbones, while her thick tawny-gold hair was uncompromisingly restrained in a ponytail. In short, she was pale, thin—and almost plain, she thought with belated indignation. It was a wonder Simon bothered with her at all.

The eyes in the mirror softened slightly. Simon was Mrs Stevens' grandson, and her own increasingly frequent escort over the last few months. She knew he was becoming fond of her—and she of him, but he made no demands on her, content to offer the companionship which, during the long lonely evenings, she so desperately craved. His parents and sister she had only met today, and she viewed with some misgiving the prospect of daily contact with them. In their eyes she was simply a member of staff and she suspected that Simon's interest in her would be tacitly discouraged.

As though her thoughts had conjured him up, there was a tap on the door and his voice called, 'Caro? Have you everything you need?'

'Come in, Simon.' She looked with affection at the tall, slightly built figure, the soft pale hair and tentative moustache. 'I've just been

2

admiring my sea view—an honour I certainly wasn't expecting!'

He smiled. 'I'm glad you like it. Actually this is my room, but I thought it would appeal to you more than one at the back.'

'Don't you mind?'

'Of course not. When we were children, Velma and I thought we were very clever nabbing the front rooms, but it turned out that the parents and Grandmother preferred those facing inland. They said they had enough of the sea during the day.'

Caroline drew a deep breath. 'I've just made a momentous decision: it's high time I stopped moping and pulled myself together. I'm surprised you haven't lost patience with me long before this.'

'You've had a rotten few months. You needed time to come to terms with it.'

'And you and your grandmother gave it to me,' she said softly. 'I'm very grateful.'

'There's nothing I wouldn't give you, Caro. I think you know that.'

She smiled, deliberately ignoring the suddenly serious note in his voice. 'So here goes! A new me is about to emerge, and the first thing to go is the ponytail!' She reached up and pulled off the toggle, shaking her hair free so that it fell in a softly curling frame round her face. 'Secondly, I'm too thin, but I've a feeling my appetite will soon return in full force, especially with French cooking to

3

tempt it. There's not much incentive when you're eating alone off a tray.' Her eyes darkened, but almost at once she laughed. 'Whoops! I shall have to watch myself. And thirdly, a spot of Mediterranean sunshine will do wonders for this sickly pallor. So you see—'

'Hey, slow down!' he protested. 'You're going too fast for me. And I liked you the way you were. You look completely different with your hair round your face like that. I hardly feel I know you!'

'You soon will. This is the real me, but it's been submerged ever since we met.'

'Well then, real Caroline, what I actually came for was to ask if you'd like to stroll down to the beach. I presume you're not going to be chained to the typewriter today?'

'No, though we'll be working to a routine most days, just like London.'

'Make sure Grandmother gives you plenty of free time. Even the Mediterranean sun won't help unless you're out in it!'

'Give me five minutes to change, then, and I'll be with you.'

As he left the room she bent quickly to the open case on the bed. When the visit to St Luc was first mentioned, Adeline Stevens had given her a cheque 'to buy what you'll need for two months in the sun'. But so totally lacking had been her interest, in clothes or anything else, that she had simply put the money in the bank and done nothing about it. Only last

4

night, when personal packing could be delayed no longer, had she piled into the suitcase the sundresses, trousers and swimsuits she'd worn in Italy the previous year.

The denim jeans were loose about the waist, but at least they were young and carefree, a world away from the plain shirts and skirts she'd been wearing almost like a uniform. And the halter-neck top, though it revealed the painful thinness of neck and shoulders would at least afford her her first medicinal dose of sunshine. She brushed her hair vigorously, pinched some colour into her cheeks and ran lightly down the stairs to the wide, open-plan hallway.

'Goodness, child! It hasn't taken you long to become acclimatised!'

Adeline Stevens emerged from the salon area, staring in amazement at the change in her self-effacing secretary.

Caroline laughed and flushed, adding still further to her transformation. 'I've decided to make the most of my stay!'

'I'm delighted to hear it.' The shrewd grey eyes went over her slight figure assessingly. 'You need more meat on your bones, my dear, but I don't doubt we'll soon achieve that. Off you go, then. Young Simon's waiting on the terrace.'

The sunshine fell across her bare shoulders like a warm shawl. Caroline paused, letting her eyes grow accustomed to the glare. The perfume from the bank of flowers rose to her nostrils in dizzying sweetness, and beyond the garden a deep hum heralded the approach of a speedboat which clove the water towing a stick figure on waterskis. Simon took her arm.

'You weren't joking about the new image!'

'Do you approve?'

'It'll take some getting used to! Yes, of course I do, if it means you're happy again.'

'How could I not be, in this gorgeous place?'

They went together down the flight of steps. 'Old Gaston waters this grass every evening,' Simon remarked, 'which is why it's still green. In another month or so it'll be an uphill battle to keep it from scorching in the sun.'

'Do the Perriers live here all year round?' asked Caroline.

'In the annexe, yes. Mind you, there's usually someone at the villa. Grandmother knows hundreds of people and they're all free to make use of it when we're not here. Or even when we are!' he added with a laugh. 'It's open house and there aren't many evenings when there's just the family sitting down to dinner. Incidentally, the pool's over there, behind that screen of trees. Very plush, with changing rooms and a bar, no less! We'll sample the facilities tomorrow!'

'Do you always spend your summers here?'

'Yes, though Grandmother only comes for May and June—after that, it's too hot for her.

And this is the last year I'll be able to stay so long. From now on I'll be limited to two or three weeks, like Father. What a ghastly prospect!'

'I suppose the other villa owners do the same thing? You must know most of them.'

'Certainly everyone along this stretch of coast. That's half the fun; there are lots of parties, picnics and so on. Some of the villas are really luxurious and you'll recognise a lot of famous faces.'

'Who, for instance?'

'Well, there's Paul and Felicity Grant—they often pop in—and Marguerite Collière, and our nearest neighbour is Giles Guthrie. You probably—'

'*Giles Guthrie?*'

Caroline dropped his arm abruptly, wide eyes flying to his face.

'His T.V. programme was quite a cult last winter. You must have seen him. He interviews people in the news getting a completely different slant—'

'Giles Guthrie is *here*?'

'I should think so. He usually is while we are.' Simon frowned. 'What's the matter? Is something wrong?'

She was still staring at him wildly, willing him to unsay his last few words. Without warning her precarious new-found happiness had shattered into a thousand fragments. That she should have come so far, seem to be given a chance to forget, only to find—

She realised that Simon was regarding her with growing consternation and forced herself to appear natural. 'Sorry, it was a—surprise. I mean, someone as famous as that, so close,' she finished lamely.

Simon gave a short laugh. 'He'll be close all right, if Velma has anything to do with it.' He bent to peer into her averted face, adding teasingly, 'You'll have plenty of opportunity to ask for his autograph!'

'I don't want it!' she said violently, adding more calmly as she saw his surprise. 'I—don't like him, I'm afraid.'

'I'm not all that struck on him myself. Too damn confident, to my way of thinking. Still, he's amicable enough, and since Velma's all over him we'll just have to make the best of it. He's brilliant at his job, you have to admit that.'

'He destroys people,' she said in a low voice.

'Oh, that's a little strong, surely? He certainly gives them a good going-over, but if they're in the news they have to expect it.'

She said abruptly, 'Simon, I want to go back to the house.'

'But we haven't even got to the beach yet!'

'I'm sorry, I—came out without my sunglasses. I'm not used to this strong light and it's giving me a headache.'

Immediately he was all concern. 'Of course, love. I should have thought to warn you.'

He took her arm again and they began to retrace their steps, more quickly this time, since Caroline set the pace. As they went up the steps on to the terrace she said hurriedly, 'I think I'll go and lie down for a while. It's probably the after-effects of the flight. What time is dinner?'

'Not till about nine; you've plenty of time. Would you like an aspirin or anything?'

'No, I'll be fine.' She was edging away from him, unsure how much longer her control would last. 'I'll see you later, then.' And she ran across the hall and up the stairs, conscious of him standing looking after her.

In the sanctuary of her room she stood with her hands to her face, trying to hold down the trembling which shook her. So the past had followed her after all; she was not to be allowed to forget. Giles Guthrie, of all people! Had she known there was the slightest risk of meeting him, she'd have abandoned her wonderful job, the months here in France, everything.

Slowly she took her hands from her face, eyes focussing on her reflection across the room: jeans, sun-top, hair soft round her face. The new image Caroline—or rather, the return of the old one. Was she going to allow Giles Guthrie, who had robbed her of so much, wipe out this tentative revival too? At least he didn't know who she was—and nor, thank goodness, did her employer. She'd told both Mrs Stevens and Simon that her father had died, but not who he had been.

Distractedly she began to walk about the room, lifting things and putting them down again. Outside the sun still shone unremittingly, but its brilliance was clouded for her now. Her confidence was rapidly evaporating and she didn't know how to hold on to it. It was so unfair that when—

Her head snapped up. Hadn't she just resolved to stop feeling sorry for herself? This was the first challenge, and though admittedly it was a far greater one than she could ever have anticipated, she had no intention of letting it floor her. She had not permitted herself to think of Giles Guthrie for six long months, clamping down instantly on memories too painful to be borne. Now she realised it was necessary, one last time, to go over what had happened. Only after such an exorcism would she be capable of meeting him face to face, as it seemed she must.

She moved to the window and sat on the wide, cushioned seat. The waterskier was still cleaving the solid-seeming blue of the sea, the spume of spray behind him glinting like a shower of diamonds in the sunshine. As she watched him her gaze slid inwards and her mind filled instead with the image of her father, kindly, gentle, with the almost fanatical gleam of the idealist in his eyes.

McDermott Cain had been a brilliant man

10

by any standards, but all his life idealism overrode practicality and in the end it was his undoing. He had always been passionately on the side of the under-dog and had won prizes for outstanding novels which drew attention to the plight of people in distress, much as Charles Dickens had done some hundred years earlier. And all his life he had had one dream constantly before him, to set up a home for delinquent boys and by gentleness, trust and example, woo them back to respectable society.

His wife had died when their daughter was ten years old, and although money was put by to complete Caroline's education, any surplus was unfailingly set aside towards this ultimate goal. When the film rights of his last novel were sold, he at last had enough capital to put the dream into effect.

Predictably, it failed. Though warned repeatedly to exercise stricter discipline, he persisted with his policy of trust and inevitably it rebounded on him. It was discovered that the boys had formed themselves into a highly organised gang of robbers, using his unwitting protection as a blind to their activities. When at last he was forced to question them, they beat him up and wrecked the house he had so lovingly put together for their benefit. Furthermore, it took the police over three months to track down the last of them, by which time all the stolen property had been disposed of.

It was at this point that Giles Guthrie invited McDermott Cain to appear on his programme. Caroline had argued vehemently against his accepting.

'He'll tie you in knots, Daddy! You know how he can twist things!'

'Nonsense, dear. It'll give me a chance to put in a word for the boys. If people realised the kind of homes they came from—'

'Oh, Daddy,' she had said despairingly, 'will you never learn?'

She remembered, sitting there in the warm sunshine, that when she had switched on the television that night, she had never been more conscious of the fierce, protective love she felt for that spare figure, so bravely waiting to put his case to a hostile public. And to the arch-enemy, his interviewer Giles Guthrie. How suave the man was! As Simon had said, how overbearingly self-confident!

'Do you not agree, Mr Cain, that brands of do-goodery such as yours often do more harm than good?'

'I can't accept that, no. If there is any way of helping—'

'But your boys duped you, didn't they, from first to last? Surely you see how they must have laughed at what they considered your gullibility?'

Two bright spots of colour had appeared on her father's face. 'Very likely, Mr Guthrie, but

12

I'd rather suffer a little ridicule than fail to—'

'And it now appears that you knew of these offences several days before you informed the police. Wasn't that irresponsible in the extreme? By holding back you not only allowed the culprits to escape and denied your neighbours the chance of recovering their property, but caused vast sums of public money to be spent on the subsequent search.'

Cain said with difficulty, 'I had to offer them one last chance to give themselves up and return what they had stolen.'

'Which,' Giles Guthrie's voice was sardonic, 'no doubt they promised to do?'

'Yes.'

'And do you, with hindsight, feel now that your action was justified?'

McDermott Cain leaned forward to take a sip from the glass in front of him, and Caroline remembered achingly how his hand had shaken.

'I do,' he said then. 'I'd do the same again.'

Giles Guthrie leaned back in his chair, the tips of his fingers pressing against each other. 'I put it to you, Mr Cain,' he said quietly, 'that possibly your action wasn't quite as altruistic as you'd have us believe. Wouldn't it in fact have been a considerable face-saver for yourself if the boys had voluntarily returned their loot? Wasn't that the real reason why you gambled with justice, to salvage your pride?'

There followed a long silence. Then Cain

13

said, with the first hint of bitterness his daughter had ever heard in his voice, 'You're very astute, Mr Guthrie, and I don't doubt you're right. I can only say I wasn't aware at the time of my own—duplicity.'

Guthrie made a slight movement and it was obvious he was disconcerted. 'I'm not accusing you of duplicity, Mr Cain. I—' And then, branded for ever on Caroline's memory, a look of concern crossed his face as, off camera, the other man jerked in sudden pain. The cameras panned back in time to catch McDermott Cain falling forward across the table and cutting his head on the breaking glass that had held the water.

And that was all. He had died in the ambulance on the way to hospital.

Caroline found that silent tears were raining down her face. Oh, Daddy, she thought piteously, how *can* I be polite to him, after what he did to you?

She moved at last, went through to the bathroom and, cupping her hands under the tap, repeatedly splashed the stingingly cold water over her face. Then, keeping her mind a careful blank, she unpacked her case and put things neatly away in the drawers and cupboards provided. It was a pleasant room, and the bathroom *en suite* was a luxury she had not expected. Simon said every room had one. Finally she had a leisurely bath, hoping that the warm, scented water would wash away the

14

sharp pain of her memories and leave only the gentle ache she could bear.

It was time to go downstairs. She selected a dress in coral linen that hugged her small waist before widening into a full skirt, its tiers slotted with broderie anglaise. But the warmth of its colour accentuated her pallor and for the first time in months she opened the make-up case which she had only included in her luggage as an afterthought. With a few skilful strokes, all signs of her recent tears were obliterated and lips and cheeks glowed with soft colour. She was presentable again.

No one was in the salon, and Caroline went through the open patio doors on to the terrace. The sun was off the front of the house now and she moved round the corner to catch the last of its dying rays. On this side, the terrace had been extended to form a wide paved patio. There was an inbuilt barbecue and, against the wall of the house, a table and several chairs.

She sat down, leaning against the warm wall and gazing out across the date palms and cacti to the slope of the hill, clothed with the dark green of young vines. In the grass below the terrace the grasshoppers were chirruping loudly.

'Giles darling! How marvellous to see you!'

Caroline shot upright, head spinning from side to side before she realised that the laughing voice, which belonged to Simon's mother, had come from the open window just above her.

And then the voice she would never forget, with the deep, caressing note that was present even when the words it spoke were barbed. 'Hello, Lydia. Welcome back to France.'

'Giles has been here two whole weeks already.' Velma this time. 'He's browner than I am, and I resent it!'

'You'll stay to dinner, of course?'

'I should be delighted, if it won't be stretching the numbers.'

'No, we've not seen anyone else yet. There'll just be the six of us—and Caroline, of course.'

Hot with embarrassment, Caroline wondered how she could escape. If she stood up, she would be visible to the group just inside the room.

Giles's voice was idle. 'And who is Caroline?'

'Mother's little typist. She came over with us this afternoon.'

'And she eats *en famille?* Isn't that rather limiting?'

Lydia laughed. 'My own feeling, but Mother's quite protective about her.'

'I can imagine. Just like Adeline to consider the hired help!'

'Simon's got a thing about her, too,' Velma added carelessly. 'Though lord knows what he sees in her—she's a mousy little creature.'

'Darling, run upstairs, would you, and see

16

what's keeping your father? I want him to take a photograph before the sun goes any lower. We always do, you know, the first evening. Meanwhile I'll go and ask Berthe to lay another place at dinner.'

As the two of them moved away Caroline rose swiftly to her feet. Only Giles Guthrie remained there now, and with luck he'd be looking the other way long enough for her to slip past both windows and reach the front door. But as she rounded the corner of the house she came face to face with him; he had stepped out of the patio door as she had herself minutes earlier. She stopped abruptly, face flaming.

'Good evening,' he said formally, mocking eyes moving over her and noting her discomfort. 'I don't believe we've met?'

She lifted her chin and met his eyes defiantly. 'I'm no one of any importance, Mr Guthrie—only the hired help.'

His eyebrows lifted. 'Oh dear,' he said unrepentantly. 'You overheard our conversation.'

'Quite unintentionally. I was on the terrace.'

'You're right to be annoyed. It was a patronising remark and I apologise. You're— Caroline, presumably?'

'Caroline Cain.' She watched him closely, but there was no flicker of response. It was a common enough name.

'Giles Guthrie, as you seemed to gather.

17

How do you do?' He held out his hand and she hesitated. Short of downright rudeness, she had no option but to take it. It was large and cool, and grasped hers firmly.

'Is this your first visit to France?'

'To this part, but I know other areas quite well.'

'Really? Where?'

'Paris and Normandy, mainly.'

'Giles?' Velma came swiftly out to join them, stopping short in surprise at Caroline's changed appearance.

'Miss Cain and I have been getting acquainted,' Giles said smoothly. 'I must say, Velma, this is some mouse!' Velma shot him a startled glance and he added, 'She overheard us earlier, I'm afraid.'

The other girl's eyes went minutely over Caroline and she didn't seem too pleased with what she saw. 'You look entirely different,' she said accusingly. 'How have you managed it?'

Caroline shrugged. 'I adapt to my environment! Excuse me.' And, head held high, she passed between them into the house. It was hardly fair, she reasoned, to blame Velma for her wholly justified opinion. How beautiful she was herself, and how different from Simon, with that straight, blue-black hair and the sensuous fullness of her mouth. No wonder Giles Guthrie was a frequent visitor.

Simon met her in the hall. 'Is your head better? You look rather flushed.'

18

'I've just had the doubtful pleasure of meeting Mr Guthrie.'

'Oh. Well, don't let him bother you. Can I get you a drink?'

'No, thank you.'

'Simon!' It was Lydia Betts from the terrace. 'Hurry up, your father's waiting to take the ceremonial photo!'

'This is a fad of Mother's,' explained Simon. 'A formal group on the terrace on the first and last night here, no matter what happens in between! Come on.'

'You don't want me in it.'

'Of course we do! You're part of the household, aren't you? More entitled to be included than Giles, come to that.'

'Please, Simon. I'd rather not,' pleaded Caroline.

'Simon!'

'Coming!' He turned back to Caroline. 'All right, if you're sure. But don't disappear again, dinner's almost ready.'

She followed him slowly, standing well back in the room and watching the group on the terrace as they laughingly arranged and rearranged themselves for the photograph. There was Adeline Stevens, with her short grey hair and sharp eyes, and Lydia, thin, dark and muscular from all the sport she played. And her husband Humphrey manipulating the camera. He was a small, dapper man, a well-known barrister whose name frequently

19

appeared in the press. And Simon, of course, and dark, lovely Velma. And Giles Guthrie.

No longer able to keep away from him, her eyes went minutely over the tall, elegant figure leaning so carelessly against the stone balustrade. A lean, clever face, with those probing blue eyes vivid in the tanned skin and dark hair growing in sideburns on either side of his head. He was wearing a mustard-coloured jacket, immaculately cut, and a silk cravat the identical colour was tucked nonchalantly into the open neck of his white shirt.

As though feeling her scrutiny, his amused eyes slid sideways from the camera lens to the open window and her motionless figure inside. 'Some mouse!' he had said, and Caroline felt a flicker of gratification. At least he hadn't seen her pale and cowed as, incredibly, she had been only this afternoon, still crushed by the blow he had unknowingly dealt her. If she had to meet Giles Guthrie in the course of her stay here, at least it would be on her own terms.

*   *   *

The dining-room was in effect the far end of the salon but on a lower level and approached by a few steps the width of the room. Its outside wall was nearly all glass which slid back to give access to the wide patio and on the opposite side of the room a door connected directly with the kitchen. Through this,

20

Madame Perrier and her solid daughter Yvette came to serve them. The plates for all the courses were piled, French fashion, one on top of each other at each place setting, and the smell of new bread rose from the basket of *petits pains* in the centre of the table.

It all felt very strange to Caroline. She had never eaten formally with the family before, and she was acutely conscious of Giles Guthrie across the table.

'What are you working on at the moment, Adeline?' he enquired, helping himself to more salad. 'It must be engrossing, for you to bring it here with you; an innovation, surely?'

'True. Usually I'm between books at this time of the year, and halfheartedly gathering material for the next one. But what with Mary unexpectedly having to leave, and the hunt for a new secretary, I'm rather behind schedule this year. Since I couldn't bear to postpone coming to France, I decided to finish it here.'

'Which must be quite a bonus for your new secretary.' There was a smile in his voice which invited Caroline to look up, but she kept her eyes steadfastly on her plate and Simon said with a touch of satisfaction, 'I'm afraid you're in Caroline's bad books, Giles.'

'Oh? I thought we'd cleared that up?'

'Cleared—? I'm not sure what you mean, but we were discussing your programme earlier. She objects to the way you—what was the word?—"destroy" your guests.'

21

'*Destroy*, Miss Cain? I doubt if their susceptibilities are as tender as yours.'

'You can be ruthless Giles,' put in Adeline unexpectedly. 'You've had me squirming in my chair more than once, watching your victims under fire.'

'Nonsense, Mother.' Humphrey Betts patted his moustache with his table napkin. 'If one is in the public eye, one is bound to get a bit of stick. Part and parcel of the thing. Have to be prepared for it.'

'Of course you do,' Velma agreed swiftly. 'And Giles is a brilliant interviewer.'

Giles's voice was carefully neutral. 'You still haven't told me, Adeline, the theme of your book?'

As Mrs Stevens began to outline the plot, Caroline at last felt able to look up. To her consternation, however, it was to find Giles Guthrie's blue, blue eyes consideringly on her. Though she had not spoken, it had been her opinion that had caused the slight contretemps and she imagined he was not too pleased by it.

However, the impression was fleeting. Almost at once he recovered his good humour and she was forced to witness a side of his character she had not known—had not wished to know—existed: that of a charming, cultivated man relaxed and at his ease among friends. Somehow she had foolishly imagined him permanently confined to the small square box that was his forum.

22

The long-drawn-out meal ended at last and, thankfully, Caroline murmured a general 'Goodnight' and slipped from the room. Simon followed and caught up with her on the stairs.

'You are all right, Caro? You seem in a strange mood tonight.'

She made herself smile at him. 'Yes, I'm fine. Just tired.'

'Sleep well, then.' He bent to kiss her cheek and as she turned to continue up the stairs, she saw that the others had also come out of the dining-room and no doubt witnessed the scene. With burning cheeks she hurried to her room.

CHAPTER TWO

Caroline woke early the next morning with the sun streaming into her room and lay for some time listening to the gulls over the water. She must remember to close the shutters before going down to breakfast, or the room would become unbearably hot.

She stretched luxuriously, still scarcely able to realise she was in this country she loved so much, with two long months stretching ahead of her. And, unbidden, Giles Guthrie's face came into her mind, obliterating everything else. Impatiently she sat up and swung her feet to the floor. Even Paradise had its serpent! she told herself with grim humour as she went to run the bath.

When she reached the breakfast table formally attired for her day's work, Adeline Stevens regarded her with a smile. 'No need for that here, child. Jeans and sun-top are perfectly good working clothes for this neck of the woods!'

'I'll change later, then,' Caroline said gratefully, accepting a warm croissant.

'We won't be starting any new work on the book today. I want to go over the last chapter again and sort one or two things out. After that, the rest of the day's your own. The routine will be much less rigorous while we're here and you must take the opportunity to relax and soak up some sunshine. You were looking quite haunted in London, you know.'

'It's very kind of you,' Caroline murmured.

'I was hoping the change would help you, but you've responded much more quickly than I expected. It must have taken courage—I admire you for it.' Adeline paused and shot the girl a look from under her eyebrows. 'What does Simon think of the transformation?'

Caroline dimpled. 'He said it would take a bit of getting used to.'

'I can imagine,' Adeline returned drily. 'My grandson is a conservative young man. He doesn't take kindly to—surprises.'

Footsteps sounded in the hall and Simon came down the steps, followed a moment later

24

by his sister.

'Simon, that was Val Parkes on the phone. She's invited us over to their villa for the day. Tennis while it's cool enough, then just lazing.'

Simon hesitated and glanced at Caroline, but before he could speak, his grandmother announced, 'My secretary is engaged this morning, I'm afraid, so she can't join you, if that's what you were about to suggest.'

'She's not invited anyway,' Velma said flatly, and there was a nasty little silence.

'Come along, Caroline.' Adeline rose to her feet. 'If you've finished, I'll show you where I'm proposing to work. And you two—the little salon is now out of bounds. It's the only room downstairs with a door I can close behind me, and this summer it will become my study.' She led the way over the cool tiled hall to a door at the far right-hand corner. 'I asked Gaston to put your typewriter and files in here, and he's bringing down the little table I normally have in my bedroom. It should be just the right height, I think.'

The small room was cool at this time of day. It had windows in two walls, one looking out on the ground behind the house, with the garage and the Perriers' annexe just visible, and the other, with the obligatory sliding windows, giving on to the terrace and beyond it a slope of garden and the trees where Simon had told her the pool was.

The next few hours passed pleasantly.

Caroline loved her work. Having admired her employer's books long before she met her, she found it fascinating to see the creative process in action, and it was a constant marvel to her how seemingly unrelated threads were constantly being woven into the complicated pattern which formed the plot. Deft touches of characterisation, telling snippets of description, a deep understanding of human reactions—all these were an integral part of Adeline Stevens' art.

They went together over the chapter they had finished just before leaving London. There were parts of it that didn't satisfy their author and each sentence was hammered until it achieved the required shape. Then Adeline retired to an armchair with a pile of notes to prepare the groundwork on the next chapter which was necessary before she could start dictating. It was a joke among her family that she only required a secretary because her handwriting was illegible even to herself. Meanwhile, Caroline swiftly sorted her own papers into serviceable piles, uncovered her typewriter, and set it up ready for use when required.

She was surprised to discover how late it was when a tap on the door heralded Gaston Perrie bearing their lunch on a tray.

'I thought we might as well have it informally in here, since the rest of them are out anyway. As you know, I eat very little in the middle of the day, but—' with a smile—'if your appetite is returning, we can always arrange for you to have something more substantial.'

'This looks delicious,' Caroline said. There were succulent pink rounds of salami, a *baguette* of still-warm bread and a selection of cheeses. Accompanying them was a bottle of Vichy water and a bowl of fresh fruit.

'After we've eaten,' Adeline continued, 'we'll finish for today. The heat at this time of the day is too much for me and I retire to my room during the afternoon. When we get properly into our routine, I propose to work from about nine till twelve, and then again at four or five o'clock for a couple of hours. Once you're up to date with your typing the rest of the time will be your own, and of course you'll be free at weekends. So, how do you propose to spend your first afternoon?'

'Would it be all right if I went to the pool?'

'An admirable idea.'

Accordingly an hour or so later, armed with her swim things, a paperback and a bottle of sun-cream, Caroline walked across the grass to the screen of pine trees. The pool, incredibly blue, lay in the centre of a wide paved sunbathing area. To one side there was a row of wooden changing cabins with a shower cubicle at each end, and on the other, resplendent under an awning, the bar about which she had thought Simon was teasing her. To her relief it was boarded up and deserted.

27

She had no wish to lie out under the gaze of Monsieur Perrier or his bold-eyed son Jules. At the far side of the pool, ensuring its complete privacy, a group of orange and lemon trees clustered close together, their fruit already visible among the branches.

Caroline changed quickly, spread her towel on the burning paving stones and rubbed cream all over her body. Then, with a sigh of pure contentment, she lay back and closed her eyes. The sun beat down and she gave herself up to its benison, consciously soaking in its life-giving heat. She had always tanned quickly and painlessly, and already there was a faint wash of honey-gold over her skin.

Away on the main road two cars passed each other at speed with a typically French blaring of horns. Then there was silence again and she slept—slept until a shadow moved between her and the sun and she came fumblingly awake to see the tall figure of Giles Guthrie looking down at her.

'The prickly Miss Cain, no less! Sorry if I disturbed you. I'm looking for Velma.'

He was wearing blue swimming trunks and a towel was slung round his neck. His body, strong, muscular and smooth-chested, was a uniform tan all over. Caroline swallowed nervously.

'She and Simon have gone over to some friends—the Parkes, I think she said.'

'Simon's deserted you? Too bad!'

28

She flushed and answered steadily, 'I've been working with Mrs Stevens all morning.'

'Isn't that surface rather hard to lie on? There are some sun chairs in the far cubicle. I don't suppose they've been out yet this year, but I could bring one over if you like.'

'I'm quite comfortable, thank you.'

He shrugged. 'Suit yourself. Well, I was hoping for a swim. Something's gone wrong with my filter and I've had to get the workmen over. Would you mind if I went ahead?'

'Of course not.' She felt behind her for book and sun-cream and he said quickly,

'You're not going to run away, are you? I'd have thought this place was big enough for both of us, but if it isn't I'll be the one to leave.'

'I—really should be getting back.'

'Why? You're not working again today, are you?'

'No, but—'

'Then for heaven's sake lie down and stop making me feel so unwelcome.' And with that he slung his towel on the ground beside her and almost in one movement dived into the water.

Caroline found she was trembling again. Why did he always have this effect on her? No, she knew the reason. Resentfully she watched as he swam effortlessly through the water, lazily varying his strokes and occasionally turning on to his back. Then, catching his eye, she hastily put on her sunglasses and opened her book, not looking up when, ten minutes or so later, he reappeared, dripping, beside her, spread out his towel and lay down. She realised belatedly that she was reading a page she'd been over at least three times already, and quickly turned it.

'You really do dislike me, don't you?' he remarked conversationally. 'I thought at first it was due to that stupid remark you overheard, but according to Simon it dates from before that. Do you mind telling me why?'

'Does it matter?' she asked tightly. 'You must have enough fans without me.'

'I find it irritating to meet such hostility, particularly in a place where up to now I've always been welcome.'

She felt the colour flood her face. 'I'm sorry. This isn't my home and I'd no right to be rude to you.'

'I suppose that's a start, but it doesn't answer my question. Since we only met yesterday, I'm at a loss to know what I've done.'

'Simon told you.'

'Prejudged by television? Isn't that a trifle naïve?'

'Perhaps I am naïve, but I happen to believe people should be allowed to keep their basic dignity, rather than have it torn from them in shreds to gratify your public.'

'A sharp tongue, forsooth! So it really was all that rubbish about hurting people's feelings? Sanctimonious claptrap! With respect,

30

of course.'

Caroline spun round angrily, but he was lying on his back with his eyes closed and his face was expressionless.

'You're not being fair!' she said hotly. 'You've just reminded me that I'm not in any position to say what I really—'

'Be my guest, though I warn you, if it's just a repetition of mealy-mouthed platitudes I shall probably fall asleep in the middle.'

'You really are insufferable, aren't you?' she burst out. 'Not least for having the conceit to be surprised anyone could dislike you! Has it never occurred to you that not everyone relishes the sight of someone being humiliated? That we don't all worship you from afar and tell ourselves how clever, how witty and pungent you are?'

Some time during this tirade he had opened his eyes and was watching her, one hand shielding his face from the sun.

'You know, you look quite delectable when roused. Pity you're such a self-righteous little prig!'

She started to rise, but his hand encircled her wrist, holding her immobile.

'Never mind the outrage, we'll take that as read. Does Simon know what a spitfire you can be? I'd have thought you'd be too much for him to handle, but no doubt he only sees the meek, unassuming little secretary we had at the dinner table, so obviously in need of his

31

protection. Very clever, Miss Cain. A ploy as old as the hills, but clever none the less. And clearly it works. You have Simon exactly where you want him, and no doubt he'll be only too willing to marry you and keep you in comfort for the rest of your days. I wish him joy of you!'

With a last wrench she succeeded in freeing herself. She scrambled to her feet and without stopping to collect her things, walked with as much dignity as her brief bikini allowed round the screen of trees. Once out of his sight she started to run, not stopping until she reached the terrace. Fortunately there was no one about and she rushed up to her room and flung herself on the bed, heart pounding, lungs straining for air, and mind a seething turmoil of fury and hatred.

She hadn't been playing a part last night, as he'd accused her, but he had: the suave, charming man-about-town on vacation. Just now the mask had been stripped away and all his basic cruelty came to the surface. How futile to have imagined she would ever be able to face him with composure!

When, finally, she was calm enough to return downstairs, it was to find her towel neatly folded on the hall table, with sunglasses, book and sun-cream laid on top of it. She stopped abruptly and Gaston, en route for the dining-room, paused.

'Monsieur Guthrie handed them in, *mademoiselle.* He said you left them at

32

the pool.'

'*Merci, monsieur.*'

'Caro? I thought I heard you. What kind of day have you had?'

Simon came out of the salon and slipped an arm round her waist. She *hadn't* been deceiving him! She really was fond of him, and her pale quietness had been all too genuine. But how could she explain, defend herself to Giles Guthrie of all people?

She said flatly, 'Quite pleasant.' A lie! 'I worked with your grandmother this morning and then went down to the pool.'

'Have a good swim?'

'Actually I didn't.' Giles had robbed her of that.

'You've caught the sun, anyway. Mind you don't overdo it.'

To Caroline's relief Giles did not appear for dinner, but unwillingly she had to admit that the meal lacked the sparkle his presence had given it the previous evening. All right, so he could be attractive and amusing—but lethal, for all that.

Over dessert Velma said, 'Have you fixed the date for the party, Grandmother? Val was asking this afternoon.'

'Not finally. One day next week, I expect.' Adeline turned to Caroline. 'We always have a housewarming soon after we arrive. Jules Perrier belongs to a group of musicians and they come and play for us to dance. It's rather

33

fun and since everyone round about is invited, it's a chance for people to meet each other. You'll enjoy it, I'm sure.'

'I haven't anything to wear for a party,' Caroline said hesitantly.

'Well, you've plenty of time to look round. I doubt if anyone will be in long dresses this year.'

By the time they rose from the table darkness had fallen. It was warm and very still.

Simon put his hand under her elbow. 'Come for a walk. I've hardly seen you all day.'

They went together through the open front door and turned in the direction of the pool, Caroline firmly closing her mind to the memories it held for her. The air was heavy with the residue of the day's sunshine, spicy from the herbs that Berthe Perrier grew along the pathways.

'If we go down to the end of the garden we come to the beach. We can walk along to St Luc and perhaps have a coffee there.'

They went slowly, hand-in-hand, and Caroline tried to anchor her thoughts on the young man at her side. What had Giles meant when he said Simon would have difficulty handling her? She pulled herself up short, resolving furiously to pay no attention to anything Giles Guthrie might say.

The colours of the flowers had merged into pale patches in the darkness, but their heady scent rose on the night air and Caroline breathed it in voluptuously. Spiky cacti and palm-tree fronds etched their exotic silhouettes against the paler blackness of the sky as they came to a long flight of steps leading down to the beach. Caroline saw that they were in a small bay only a few hundred yards across and bounded on each side by high craggy cliffs.

'When the sea's rough,' Simon told her, this bay's completely cut off. We consider it our private beach, since only Giles's villa and ours have direct access to it.'

They turned and began to walk along the sand. To their right, the unseen darkness of the sea rustled and murmured in its sleep, while on the left scrubby trees and bushes bordered the shoreline, interspersed with the sweet-smelling herbs which grow in wild profusion over southern France.

Once they had rounded the outcrop of rocks, the lights of St Luc were visible ahead of them and as they approached the little port, music from the open-air cafés drifted towards them. At the end of the beach a rocky promontory swept round the coastline, forming a natural protective barrier encircling the harbour. On this outer side, steps had been hewn out of the buttress and these they climbed, emerging from the blue silence of the beach into the noise and bright lights of St Luc.

Though it was early in the season, its narrow

streets were thronged with holiday crowds. Shops were still open, displaying expensive goods among the trish-trash of souvenirs, and Simon and Caroline mingled with the crowds, searching the endless racks of postcards for views they recognised and admiring the wide variety of merchandise on offer.

After a while they stopped at one of the pavement cafés and sat watching the continually passing crowd, mostly girls and boys with arms wound lovingly round each other.

And all at once Caroline was aware of a lump in her throat and a sense of numbing loneliness. She had Simon, she reminded herself swiftly, but was Simon what she wanted? His kisses, light and ineffectual, had not stirred her at all, though she knew he was fond of her. Perhaps he was deliberately holding back for her sake?

'You're very quiet,' he said softly, closing his hand over hers on the table.

'So are you,' she countered.

'Sorry. It's so good to be with you and yet feel we don't have to talk all the time.' He hesitated. 'I missed you very much today. I kept wondering what you were doing.'

She did not reply. The lantern above her shone down on her hair, its golden lights more noticeable after the afternoon's sunshine, and on the soft line of cheek and throat. Two boys walking past whistled appreciatively, and

36

Simon frowned and stood up.

'Shall we start back?'

'If you like.' She felt bemused, drugged with sunshine, one step from reality. The lilt of French voices, the evocative smell of garlic and Gauloises, the deep southern night kept at bay by the brave circle of harbour lights—all these things brought a sensation of happiness that was almost pain. Because there was one thing missing and she didn't know how to find it.

As they came down the worn steps on to the sand again, the lights and crowds fell away and they were wrapped once more in silence. In the shadows of the rock, two figures were locked together, the man's arms tightly round the girl, her back arched against them. Caroline quickly turned her head away and stumbled on beside Simon. The faint breeze off the sea was warm and salty on their faces and Simon's hand held tightly to hers. She bent and slipped off her sandals, carrying them in her free hand swinging from their straps. The sand was cool and silky between her toes, occasionally pockmarked where during the day some child had been digging. It was a grey-white wilderness, drained of colour in the starlight, and they might have been walking the shores of the moon's tideless seas.

'I love you, Caro,' Simon said suddenly, and so bewitched was she by the magic of the night that his voice came as a shock and it was a moment before the meaning of his words reached her. Even then she had no way to answer him.

'I wanted you to know,' he went on, 'so that you'd feel safe and cared-for. You need never be alone again.'

'Oh, Simon!' Hot tears rushed to her eyes.

He stopped and turned her gently to face him, hands on her shoulders. 'You will marry me, won't you, darling?'

'I—don't know,' she faltered.

'I thought you loved me too?'

'I do—oh, I do—in a way. I'm not sure if it's enough. I don't want to short-change you, Simon.'

He smiled. 'Let me worry about that. These last few months have drained you of emotion. It's not surprising you haven't had any to spare, but it'll come in time. Meanwhile as long as you love me "in a way", that's fine. I've enough for both of us.'

She said with a catch in her voice, 'Kiss me, Simon.'

But when his lips touched hers, they were as soft and undemanding as a butterfly's wing and she was aware of a sharp ache of disappointment. Surely there must be more than this? Or were all the love songs in the world part of one gigantic hoax?

Remembering the couple by the rock, she let her sandals fall and reached up, taking hold of his head between her hands and drawing it down to her waiting mouth. But almost at once he gently moved back.

'No, darling,' he said jerkily, 'not that way. It's no use trying to hurry it.'

But I wasn't! she cried silently. I was just trying to discover if there's anything there! Disconsolately she bent to retrieve her shoes and with his arm round her shoulders they resumed their walking, rounding the protruding cliff-face into their own little bay.

So what had been decided? she thought in confusion. She hadn't accepted him, nor turned him down, but he seemed satisfied with the outcome. Did he consider they were engaged? And if so, how would his family react? She doubted if his parents would approve, and Velma certainly didn't like her. Only Mrs Stevens would be her ally. Was Simon strong enough to go against his parents' wishes?

Giles Guthrie, of course, would complacently assume that his judgment of her had been correct. And remembering Giles, she realised she'd left her clothes in the changing-room by the pool.

They reached the steps and Simon waited while Caroline slipped on her sandals. It was as well she hadn't unfastened them, because her fingers were shaking and would not have been able to manage the buckles.

'I left my clothes at the pool,' she said as they came abreast of the trees, and her voice sounded strange after its long silence. The distance she had covered this evening seemed far greater than merely to St Luc and back, but she had not yet had time to analyse it.

Simon accompanied her into the shadows and waited while she fumbled inside the dark cubicle. The place where she had sat with Giles in blazing sunshine was cold and eerie under the stars. What was he doing now? she wondered. Certainly not thinking of her, unless he was laughing over the incident with some friends.

Lydia and Humphrey Betts were sitting smoking on the terrace. Panic-stricken, Caroline wondered if Simon would announce their engagement, but the moment passed. He stayed talking to his parents and she went alone into the silent house.

There was no denying it had been an eventful day. She slipped out of her dress and hung it in the cupboard, her mind still on Simon's proposal. If she married him, she'd never have to go back to that lonely, empty flat again. And even if they didn't approve of her, marriage would provide her with a ready-made family, which was something she craved.

Her mind flooded suddenly with the picture of the two figures under the rock straining so hungrily together. Why did Simon never kiss. her like that? Was he really checking himself out of consideration for her, or was his definition of love simply a deep caring— affection, solicitude, companionship? And was she wrong, not to be satisfied with that?

CHAPTER THREE

When Caroline reached the study the next morning, it was to find her employer more concerned with planning the housewarming party than her new novel. Guest lists had to be prepared, invitations typed, and throughout the next few days Caroline spent all her working hours ticking off names as answers were received, arranging for electricians to rig lights in the trees round the villa, and phoning agencies to engage extra staff for the evening. It seemed that work on the novel was to be postponed until after the party.

Despite all these frantic preparations, however, Mrs Stevens kept her word about allowing her plenty of free time and by the end of the week Caroline had lost all trace of the pale, drawn girl who had arrived at the villa. The hollows in neck and cheeks had filled out and her arms and legs grew rounded again. Moreover the sun, while highlighting streaks of gold in her hair, tanned her skin to a rich honey-brown and the shadows which had circled her eyes for six months finally disappeared.

The family's reaction to the change in her varied according to temperament. Mrs Stevens expressed unqualified approval, while her daughter and son-in-law ignored—or possibly didn't even notice—the difference. Velma made no comment, though several times Caroline was aware of coming under her close scrutiny, but it was Simon's reaction which surprised and rather saddened her. To her relief he had made no further mention of the possibility of their engagement, but one evening as they stood on the terrace, the low evening sunshine burnishing her hair and skin, he said almost naïvely, 'You're beautiful, Caro. I hadn't realised it before.'

Slightly embarrassed, she gave a little laugh. 'There's no need to sound so disappointed!'

But he didn't smile in reply. 'It's just that in a way you seemed lovelier to me back in London, when you were so grave and quiet and—desperate.'

'You wish I was still like that?' she asked incredulously.

'Not unhappy, of course, but now that you're bright and self-confident again you don't seem to need me as you did.'

And to that comment she could think of no adequate reply.

During this time, though there were frequently visitors round the table for dinner, there had been no further sign of Giles Guthrie, for which Caroline was thankful. She gathered from general conversation that he was spending a lot of time on his boat, which was moored in St Luc harbour, and occasionally—though possibly, Caroline suspected, not as often as she would have wished—Velma accompanied him. He had of course accepted the party invitation, but with so many people around then it should, she assured herself, be reasonably easy to avoid him.

Meanwhile she had still not bought herself a suitable dress, and one afternoon she forsook the pool and caught the local autobus to St Luc. She had not been there since the evening with Simon and was surprised to find it larger than her first impression had seemed to indicate.

The port was crowded with boats of all descriptions—one of them, no doubt, belonging to Giles—and behind the harbour narrow cobbled streets climbed the hill, twisting and turning and leading off one another in a fascinating maze. Above the shops which lined the pavements, faded blue shutters opened on strings of washing, and vivid climbing plants crept up the ochre walls. The footpaths were so narrow that in order to pass anyone it was necessary to step into the road, an imminently dangerous operation in view of the large cars which, with no concession to the lack of space, sped continually up and down.

The shops themselves fascinated her— charcuteries with bowls of mixed salads, succulent slices of ham, pies and pasties, and pâtisseries, grottoes of delight filled with glazed apple and pear flans, candied fruits, macaroons and delicate leaves of almond crisp. Each open doorway despatched its own appetising aroma to tempt her inside— roasting coffee, chickens turning on a spit, herbs and spices.

So engrossed was she by the colourful display on all sides that she had almost forgotten the purpose of her visit. But suddenly, rounding yet another corner, she found herself facing the window of a small boutique, and arranged artistically on a stand was exactly the dress she had been looking for. Nor, on anxious inspection, was the price tab beyond her means. In an excess of fear that it might not be her size, she went inside—and moments later relaxed with a deep sigh of pleasure. The dress, in pale lemon georgette, fitted her perfectly. It was sleeveless, with a deep scooped neckline at the front and a very low back which showed her newly acquired tan to maximum advantage. But the diaphanous swirling skirt proved only a token concealment for her legs.

'C'est transparent!' she exclaimed uncertainly, and the assistant laughed.

'Absolument, mademoiselle! It is designed that the legs should be visible beneath. Mademoiselle is fortunate to have good ones!'

Caroline hesitated, uneasily aware that the dress was unlikely to appeal to Simon. Yet after all, she reasoned, when she swam and sunbathed her legs had been on view to everyone. Why not also when she danced?

'I'll take it,' she said.

She emerged from the boutique hot and thirsty and decided to make her way to one of the many cafés which lined the harbour front and relax with an iced drink. She selected one at random and was threading her way through the crowded tables when to her consternation she caught sight of Giles. She stopped, intending a hasty retreat, but in the same moment he looked up and saw her. She said stiffly, 'Good afternoon,' and he nodded briefly in reply.

They both intended that to be the extent of their meeting, but Giles was sitting with a group of friends and one of them, a young man with tousled hair, turned and looked up at her, his eyes noticeably brightening.

'Well, hello! Aren't you going to introduce us, Giles?'

'Tom Fawcett, Caroline Cain.'

Caroline murmured, 'Hello' and would have moved on, but Tom caught hold of her hand.

'Hey, you're not getting away that easily! There's a spare seat—come and join us.'

'No, really, I—'

'Of course you must! Move over, Pam, there's a love.'

Across the ensuing bustle Caroline glanced at Giles, noting his compressed lips and the expression in his eyes which warned her not to join them. Its effect was instantaneous. She bestowed a dazzling smile on the admiring Tom and promptly sat down in the vacated chair beside him.

'That's better. Now, since Giles is neglecting his duty, let me introduce you all round. This is Pam, as you'll have gathered, that's Barry, his wife Stella, and Richard on your left. What are you drinking?' And he lifted a finger to a passing waiter.

'*Orange pressée,* please, but I—'

'Nonsense. *Une orange pressée, s'il vous plaît, monsieur.*' His accent, Caroline noted, was decidedly English. 'Where are you staying?'

'At the Villa Mimosa. I work there.'

'For old Adeline?'

'Yes, I'm her secretary.'

'So that's how Giles met you. I must say, old man, you're a dark horse! No doubt you wanted to keep this gorgeous creature to yourself.'

Caroline felt her lips twitch and didn't dare to look at Giles. He answered calmly, 'Perhaps I should warn you, Tom, that Simon has a prior claim there.'

'*Simon?* Old Simon, with this bird of paradise? He wouldn't know what to do with her!' He gave a snort of laughter and then glanced at Caroline a little anxiously. 'Or am I speaking out of turn? *Has* he a claim on you?'

She felt her face grow hot. 'To a certain extent,' she admitted, and seized gladly on the glass of orange juice as it was put before her.

'Well, I'm blowed! If I was going to be here any length of time I'd do my best to alter that, but unfortunately we fly home on Saturday. We won't even make the party. I was disappointed before—now I'm desolate!'

His woeful face made Caroline laugh. 'We'll drink a toast to absent friends!'

Tom began to ply her with questions which she answered automatically, glancing surreptitiously at Giles. Opting out of any involvement in their conversation, he was talking to the girl Stella on his left, lounging back in his chair with his long brown legs nonchalantly crossed. He was wearing brief navy and white shorts and his shirt was open to the waist.

'We've just been round the coast to St Tropez,' Tom was saying. 'Have you been out on Giles's boat?'

'No. Actually, I hardly know him. We've only met twice.'

'Well, you must get him to take you. And Simon, of course. She's a lovely craft, a fifteen-metre cabin cruiser. Sleeps four plus crew.'

'Oh.' Caroline hoped she sounded suitably impressed. It seemed an inadequate response, but she couldn't think of any intelligent comment to make on boats, about which she knew nothing. Instead she said, 'Are you all going home on Saturday?'

'Only Richard and I. Barry and Stella are

here for another week—and Pam, who's Stella's sister. You and Giles have it very cushy, I must say, staying for months at a time. He tries to imply he's doing freelance journalism while he's here, but I don't believe a word of it.'

'You will,' returned Giles, whose attention had been caught by his name, 'when you read my article in the *Sunday Times*!'

Caroline drained her glass and set it on the table. 'I must be going. I have to report for duty again at five. Thank you very much for the drink, I was in need of it.'

Tom stood up with her. 'Any chance of seeing you again before I go?'

'I'm afraid not. I've a lot of work to do, and anyway—'

'Simon?'

'Yes.'

'Fair enough, but I wish I'd met you first! Think of me sometime.'

Caroline smiled, took the hand he held out, and her general 'Goodbye' included them all. As her eyes swept over Giles, he was not looking in her direction.

Later that evening, in the privacy of her room, she again tried on the yellow dress and it seemed even more daring than it had in the shop. Still, it was too late to do anything about it now; it was the only possible one for her to wear at the party.

At last, in an increasing fever of

48

preparation, the great day arrived. Madame Perrier, with two women from the village to help her, was ensconced in the kitchen, from which came titillating smells of pâtés and terrines, roasting chicken and boiling ham. At the long table one of her assistants chopped an endless supply of lettuces, tomatoes, peppers and olives. Great pans of rice were drained and allowed to cool, delicate gâteaux and pastries from the pâtisserie were reverently lifted from their cardboard boxes, and the whole villa blossomed with magnificent vases of flowers.

In the late afternoon Jules Perrier and his two companions arrived to set up amplifiers to relay their music. Lydia Betts had not appeared all day; Caroline gathered she was undergoing a series of appointments with hairdresser, manicurist and masseuse. Her husband meanwhile spent most of his time gazing out of the windows and trying to predict whether or not the mistral was likely to strike.

'Do stop fussing, Humphrey!' Adeline said finally. 'There hasn't been a breath of wind all day!'

'Nor was there last year,' he answered darkly, 'until about seven o'clock, and then it blew all the lights down.'

As the hour approached, Caroline grew increasingly nervous. Was her dress really suitable for what Giles—and possibly everyone else—regarded as 'the hired help'? And the house would be full of people she didn't know. Perhaps, she thought forlornly, she could occupy herself in refilling plates and glasses—a hope that was dashed when she remembered the professional staff engaged for the purpose.

'Caroline!' It was Mrs Stevens from the hall. 'Are you nearly ready? Could you come and give me a hand?'

She took a deep breath and went running down the stairs. Simon was standing in the hall with his grandmother. Caroline saw his mouth open in surprise, but before he could speak Mrs Stevens exclaimed, 'What a fabulous dress! How lovely you look, child!' And she could have flung her arms round her in relief.

'Yes indeed,' Simon said quickly. 'It's—very striking.'

'Look, dear—' Mrs Stevens took her arm, 'I expressly told the women to lay out the dishes in the sequence we planned. They haven't, of course, and now they've moved on to other things and haven't time to rearrange them. Would you mind? You remember what we decided?'

Glad to have something to occupy her, Caroline set about her task. The open plan of the ground floor made the villa an ideal setting for parties. As she worked she could hear the sound of voices and realised that the first guests had arrived. They were being served with drinks out on the terrace. Velma appeared and went out to join them. Her

50

dress, in pale lilac, had a backline similar to Caroline's but was not, Caroline told herself, quite as pretty.

Then she had no further time to notice what people were wearing, and for a while despite the outside help she was kept busy handing round savouries and taking empty glasses to be refilled. At one stage Adeline rescued her from such tasks and took her round on her arm introducing her to people. Several times Simon sought her out, but he was usually called away almost at once by some long-lost friend who had just caught sight of him.

Caroline began to wonder with increasing anxiety at what time they would eat. She was ravenously hungry and tormented by the smells drifting across from the stacked tables in the centre of the dining-room. At last, when it was almost eleven, people began to move through and heap their plates, retreating with them to different parts of the house, terrace and garden.

Caroline found herself next to Pam, the girl from the café.

'What a heavenly dress you're wearing!' she said admiringly. 'I wish I could get away with something like that!'

'I was afraid it might be a little daring,' Caroline confessed.

'Nonsense! Very sexy but in a discreet, tantalising way! Poor old Tom would go berserk if he could see you!'

51

They sat together on the bottom step of the staircase and began to eat the dappled brawn, the firm white chicken and the colourful salads on their plates. And all the time, above the ever-rising voices, the music of Jules Perrier's trio thrummed out through the loudspeakers and, despite the wide open windows, the air grew thick with the pungent blue smoke of French cigarettes.

They finished their main course, helped themselves to *millefeuille* and fruit salad and continued chatting as they ate. Caroline learned that Barry's uncle owned one of the villas farther down the road, and a crowd of them came over every May before the owner arrived for his own holiday.

'It's perfect at this time of year,' Pam said enthusiastically, 'while there are still flowers everywhere and before the real crowds come.'

'So there you are! I've been looking for you!' Caroline looked up to see Simon in front of her. 'I was going to ask you to dance, but if you're still eating—'

'I've eaten enough!' she said ruefully, rising to her feet and laying the plate on the hall table. 'I'll come back for the rest of it later.'

The music was slower now and she wished Simon would hold her close, dance cheek-to-cheek as other couples were doing. But he held her casually at arm's length, his hand lightly clasping hers as though she were a stranger. Didn't her nearness on this warm

52

summer night mean anything to him at all?

The dance ended, someone called across to Simon and he moved away. A man came up and asked Caroline to dance. He moved well, with more dexterity than Simon's rather stiff movements. Then that dance ended too and Caroline leant back against the warm stonework. Her eyes were still smarting from the smoke and she had no wish to go inside again. However, she felt rather conspicuous out here alone. She'd retreat to the study, except for the kitchen the only room downstairs with a door of its own. It was at the far side of the house from the party and with luck the smoke might not have reached there.

She let herself in cautiously, without switching on the light. The shutters had not been closed, but no light came from outside. It was the only window opening on to the terrace at this side of the house and there were no fairy lights round here.

As she crossed the room she caught sight of a smudge of pale dress outside and stopped, thinking she might be interrupting some rendezvous. But the girl, whoever she was, moved away, and after waiting for a moment Caroline slid back the windows and stepped outside.

Out here the music from the loudspeakers was more muted and she could hear the crickets in the long grass. A faint breeze touched her hot cheeks and the scent of the

53

flowers banked along the wall rose to her nostrils with almost unbearable sweetness.

Caroline let the shadows wrap themselves round her and breathed a sigh of relief. She leaned on the stone balustrade, allowing her eyes to accustom themselves to the darkness and her thoughts to drift. She was tired, she realised, keyed up in the general excitement and yet not really part of it. If she could play a more active part in the proceedings, perhaps—

A pair of strong arms suddenly encircled her and spun her round. Lost in her dreaming, she hadn't heard anyone approaching, and before she could protest a mouth came firmly down on hers.

Almost at once she dismissed the possibility of its being Simon, for the kiss was nothing like his. It was at once teasing, masterful, lighthearted, but hinting at underlying currents. Presumably she was being mistaken for the girl who had been here minutes before. Still, this was a party after all and she'd been longing for just such a kiss. It would do no harm to poach a moment longer, and in any case, from the strength of his hold, the stranger had no intention of releasing her.

She relaxed, moving slightly and parting her lips, and immediately the whole tenor of the kiss shifted—fractionally, but with devastating results. He made some sound and opened his mouth and a sharp, sweet urgency coursed through her body, as though some nerve

54

centre, dormant until now, had sprung into quivering life. Without conscious thought she found herself clinging to him, exulting in the hard strength of his body pressing so forcefully against hers.

Her response, hesitant, inexperienced and now full of ardour, seemed to have taken her unknown lover by surprise and what had begun as an idle kiss had changed beyond belief into something exhilarating, demanding and not a little frightening. His hands moved possessively over the bare skin of her back and she quivered under their caress, a sweet, insidious helplessness drugging her senses to the point where she could think of nothing but this shared moment and the hopeless longing that it would never end.

Belatedly, though, sanity began to return and she realised the situation was rapidly getting out of hand. She put her hands flat against his chest and began to push, the pounding of his heart beneath her palms confirming that their embrace had become considerably more passionate than he had intended. And that, she thought dazedly, was because of her. The first half of the kiss had been for the unknown girl he had supposed her to be, but the latter, which had apparently taken them both by surprise, was solely for her.

It took some time before she succeeded in freeing her mouth, and as he realised her intention of escaping his hands tightened on her arms.

'Don't go!' he said urgently. 'Who in heaven's name are you?'

And she knew who he was. With an upsurge of desperation she tore herself free and went hurtling out into the blessed darkness of the garden. She heard him call after her, but her only thought was the need to keep her identity secret from him—for always. With reckless speed she went racing over the treacherous uneven, unseen grass, automatically heading, as she had so often in warm sunlight, for the sanctuary of the pool.

Only as she reached the trees did she turn, eyes straining back towards the house. No one was following her, nor, she thought with a touch of grim humour, had she lost a glass slipper during her headlong flight. There was no possible way he could identify her. And only then, as she leaned her bare back against the prickly bark of a pine tree, did she dare to consider what had happened. Even now, knowing who he was, the memory of his mouth and hands brought a wave of weakness and she sank to the ground, her yellow skirt billowing around her, burying her face in her hands.

It must have been Velma, out there before her. The darkness had blotted out the colour of her hair and Velma's lilac dress would be indistinguishable from her own, especially as each had a similar low-cut back. At what stage

56

had he realised she wasn't Velma? And why hadn't he stopped kissing her then?

But then again, why should he? Perhaps a man like Giles Guthrie took his pleasure where he found it—and certainly she had offered it to him on a plate. Her face burned in humiliation. And all, basically, because of curiosity. She had wanted to experience a passionate kiss, such as Simon refused to give her. Now, most certainly, she had, and again the contraction, pleasurable but oddly painful, moved inside her. Her body, it seemed, was uncaring of the identity of its lover. Why, she asked herself rebelliously, why, of all the men in the world, should the one who had aroused her and, let it not be forgotten, been aroused in his turn—be the hated Giles Guthrie?

He would be curious to know who she was. She sensed he was a man not used to being caught off balance, normally well able to hold his emotions in check. Her face burned again at the recollection that it had been her own response that had triggered the whole thing off.

She leaned her head against the tree, gazing back up the garden at the house. From this angle she could see the dark side of the terrace along by the study and also the brilliantly-lit front, where figures moved lazily in groups or drifted into dance. Somehow she would have to make her way back without being seen. Presumably the study window would still be open. Once among the noisy throng she would be safe, and though at the thought of seeing Giles the muscles of her stomach tightened apprehensively, at least he wouldn't realise she had been his partner in the dark.

Even with this reassurance it was several more minutes before she felt composed enough to start back. Still, Mrs Stevens might well be looking for her. She stood up reluctantly, and dusted the telltale pine needles off her dress. Then, keeping well over to the right as far as possible from the probing lights, she once more gained the terrace. As she had supposed, the window was still open, and with a thankful sigh she stepped inside.

But her relief was premature. A hand gripped her arm and a voice said purposefully, 'I think we have a little unfinished business to settle.' There was a click as the switch of the desk lamp went down and the ensuing circle of light held them pinned like flies in amber.

'*Caroline!*' She felt the shock go through him and his hand fell from her arm.

'I'm sorry,' she said helplessly.

'*Sorry?*' He gave a short laugh. 'You didn't seem "sorry" at the time!'

'I—didn't know who you were.'

'That is abundantly obvious. Yet you don't seem too surprised now.'

'I recognised you when you spoke,' she said in a low voice.

'Which was why you fled? Understandable.

58

But who the hell did you think I was? Not Simon, surely? I imagine his technique is somewhat different?'

Her head lifted at his tone. 'Why should you suppose that? I doubt if you're unique.' And at his angry movement she went on rapidly, 'Presumably you took me at first for Velma, but you didn't stop when you discovered your mistake, did you? You can't put all the blame on me.'

After a moment he said, 'I wasn't aware that *blame* came into it. Why were you so determined I shouldn't find out who you were?'

'Because I wanted to avoid precisely this. I knew you wouldn't be pleased, though you needn't worry. It's in the best of traditions to compromise the servants.'

'You won't let me forget that stupid remark, will you? Since it apparently still rankles, I apologise again, but as far as compromising goes, I think you did your own share of that!'

An undercurrent of amusement had crept into his voice and it added to her discomfort. For all his disclaimer, discovering her identity had obviously taken the heat out of his interest and he was now seeing the funny side. Who'd have thought 'the little typist' would have proved such a firebrand?

Out of a hurt she could not admit, she said furiously, 'I'm glad it proved a diversion for you, but you'll forgive me if I don't see it in the same light.'

'What light do you see it in?' he asked quietly. His eyes were moving over her, as though matching her visible presence with his memories of caresses in the dark. Despite herself Caroline couldn't suppress a little quiver, and he put a tentative hand on hers.

'Caroline, do we have to—?'

But she had recoiled, terrified at the response which leapt inside her. 'Don't touch me!' she said breathlessly. 'I've had more than enough of that. Save it for Velma—perhaps she appreciates you!' And she went quickly from the room, leaving him standing by the window in the golden pool of light.

Her sudden eruption from the drama of the secluded study to the noisy crowded hallway gave her no time for adjustment and almost at once Simon said, 'There you are! You keep disappearing! Come and dance.'

Tremblingly she allowed herself to be led outside again—to the softly lit terrace this time, round the corner by the dining-room. Through the open windows she could see the wrecked remains of the sumptuous meal that had been laid on the table. Simon's arms went lightly round her and she closed her mind forcibly on the memory of the last arms that had held her.

His eyes were on her face, 'All right, love? You seem a bit tense.'

'I'm tired, that's all. How long will the party

go on?'

He shrugged. 'One or two o'clock, I suppose. It's not worth going to bed till it finishes. There's too much noise to settle.'

'It would hardly be polite, anyway.'

'I've done all my duty dances now, so I'll be around to give you moral support.'

'I may well need it!'

He smiled and brushed his lips against her hair in a little gesture of affection. Oh, if only that passionate lover in the dark had proved to be Simon! She'd have had no doubts about marrying him then!

'Come on,' he said as the music ended. 'I'll get you a drink. When I last passed the hall table your plate of fruit salad was still there. Would you like it now?'

She shook her head. Her churning stomach seemed to indicate that it would never want food again. As they moved into the dining-room Velma came up to them.

'Simon, have you seen Giles? I can't find him anywhere.'

Her mother, over by the salon steps, came down to join them.

'He had to leave unexpectedly, darling. He sent his apologies.'

Velma frowned. 'But why, for heaven's sake? It's only about twelve-thirty, isn't it? He could at least have said goodbye.'

Lydia shrugged. 'He seemed in a hurry. No doubt he'll ring and explain.'

61

Caroline accepted the glass of wine Simon passed her, willing her hand not to tremble. At least Giles was now as anxious to avoid her as she him. Which, she told herself against the tight ache of her throat, was the way she wanted it. But her disloyal brain played back his last words in the study as he'd put a placating hand out towards her: 'Do we have to—?'

What had he been going to say when she cut him off so brutally? Not that it mattered. Nothing he might say or do altered the fact of who he was and what he had already done— to her father. That was the only thing to remember. Nothing that had happened between them could change that.

Adeline drifted towards them. 'Everyone having a good time? I think it's going very well, don't you?' And she moved on in a haze of cigarette smoke.

Remorselessly the interminable evening ground on, till Caroline felt she'd been smiling and laughing and dancing and talking in some grotesque forty-eight-hour marathon. And with each smile and laugh and dance, the happenings of earlier in the evening seemed more and more bizarre. It simply couldn't have happened—not with Giles Guthrie. It must all be some weird hallucination of this unending night.

As she reached the stage of believing the party would never finish, it suddenly did so.

The last guests departed in a flurry of laughter and thanks and at last she was free to escape. Her eyes were strained, every bone in her body ached. Carefully she slipped out of the yellow dress, hung it in the cupboard and stood for a moment looking at it before she shut the door. Would she ever wear it again, or would the memories so irrevocably attached to it prove an insurmountable barrier?

Moving like a robot, she prepared for bed and climbed wearily into it. The housewarming party was over, but she knew bleakly that during the course of it some deep, secret part of her had been changed and she would never be quite the same again.

She reached up for the light switch, the obedient darkness swooped down, and she lay rigidly waiting for the oblivion of sleep.

CHAPTER FOUR

During the next few days Caroline was aware of a deep restlessness. The work on the novel had finally begun in earnest, which meant that during the hours she spent with Adeline her mind was totally occupied—a very necessary state at the moment. But she soon found she was unable to cope with the thoughts and memories that came crowding every time she relaxed by the pool. To escape them, she formed the habit of going down to St Luc where she spent her time exploring its back alleyways and paved courtyards, though she was careful to avoid the cafés along the port where the previous week she had met Giles and his friends.

This method of escape was assisted by Lydia Betts, who had fallen into the habit of using her as a messenger.

'Are you going to the village, Caroline? Be a love and buy me some sun-cream from the *pharmacie* in the Rue des Carrons,' or, 'I've run out of cigarettes, Caroline. Have you time to slip down to the village for me?'

Adeline obviously did not approve of such tactics, and once she said shortly, 'There's no earthly reason why Caroline should run errands for you, Lydia.'

But Caroline herself, only too grateful to have something to occupy her, felt no resentment. She came to know the various shopkeepers and enjoyed using her French to pass the time of day with them. Having spent a year in Normandy with her father when she left school she spoke fluently, with no trace of an English accent. And all the time she was developing a mental censor, an iron door in her mind which clanged shut on every tentative thought of Giles Guthrie. But of course, as she had known it must, the time came when they had to meet again.

It was the following Saturday—a week

after the party—and as always at weekends Caroline was free. At breakfast, Simon said enthusiastically, 'Let's have an all-day session at the pool. We can have lunch and possibly even dinner down there—have the bar open, of course, and invite people over. Remember we did it once before, a few years ago? It was great.'

The idea was taken up with alacrity, phone calls were made and Simon refused to accept that Caroline had any business in St Luc which would prevent her joining in the festivity. She knew with dull certainty that Giles was sure to come, but she had been granted a week to regain her composure and she must be thankful for that. Nor had she the slightest intention that he should deduce the mood she had been in since their last encounter. For the sake of the rest of them as well as herself, she would have to be completely natural towards him.

She was fooling around in the water with Simon when he arrived, lying on her back and kicking furiously, her hair streaming out behind her and the black bikini moulded to her like a second glistening skin. He was wearing sunglasses so she couldn't tell if he glanced in her direction, but she noted with a sinking heart that he had chosen to sit in the far corner where she and Simon had left their things and to which they would eventually have to return. Velma, of course, was also there, and a crowd of people Caroline had met at the party. Lydia and Humphrey Betts, together with Adeline, had formed a group of their own contemporaries at the other side of the pool, and behind the gaily canopied bar Gaston Perrier was kept busy serving long, cold drinks.

It was very hot. The sky was azure blue without a cloud in it and the trees shimmered in a faint haze of heat. Around the pool bodies of all ages, shapes and sizes bared themselves to the molten golden ball of the sun. There were a fair number of French among them, as there had been at the party, but everyone spoke English. Caroline thought it a pity.

Out of the corner of her eye she saw Giles stand suddenly, strip off his towelling shirt and dive smoothly into the water. Automatically she turned on to her front and swam in the opposite direction. A second later she felt her ankles grasped and she was pulled down, down into the iridescent clarity at the bottom of the pool. She struggled furiously, but she'd had time to take a deep breath before she submerged and was in no danger of choking. The hands left her ankles, moved to her shoulders and held her down for several long, unnumbered seconds during which she opened her eyes and looked directly into Giles's face, his hair floating upwards, his eyes, unreadable, gauging her reaction. As he released her she shot upwards like a cork from the bottle, aware of his parallel progress, and they broke the surface together, wiping their faces and gasping for air.

He said very softly, 'Quits?' and, turning on his back, swam away. Slowly Caroline dog-paddled her way to the steps and heaved herself out of the water. She gave her hair a cursory rub, then spread the towel and stretched out on it, face down, feeling the hot sun on back and shoulders. A moment later Simon flopped down beside her.

'Unprovoked attack, I call that!' he said sympathetically.

No, she thought, not unprovoked. She had had the last word on the previous occasion— this was *quid pro quo.*

'Caroline?'

'Um?'

'I said do you want revenge? Shall I go after him?'

'No, leave it, Simon. Anyone in the pool is fair game, I suppose.' She closed her eyes and her mind—the latter more difficult with the fresh stimulus it had just received. Quits? Yes, she was prepared to call it that.

The sun-soaked moments passed. She was aware of those around her coming and going, slipping into the pool and returning from it. Their voices, spasmodic and disembodied, conveyed no meaning to her drowsing brain. The mental block was functioning reasonably well until Velma's voice, clear and close at hand, penetrated her lethargy.

'Be a darling, Giles, and oil my back.'

Caroline's eyes fluttered and remained resolutely closed. His voice was uncomfortably close.

'I warn you, my hands are still cold.'

Velma gave a little shriek as he began to comply. 'They certainly are! Does that mean a warm heart, my love?'

'Debatable,' said Giles.

'That's lovely—up there by my shoulder-blades, where I can't reach. There's topless bathing all round the coast, but Grandmother refuses point-blank to allow it here. "If you want to display yourself, go to St Tropez!" she said. Positively Victorian!'

'No one could accuse you of being exactly overdressed, Velma!' commented a young man Caroline recognised as Val Parkes' fiancé.

'It would be rather embarrassing, surely?' Simon said. 'I shouldn't know where to look.'

'Giles would!' Velma returned with a laugh. 'Grow up, little brother!'

Simon flushed but continued doggedly, 'You took the boat to St Tropez, didn't you, Giles? Barry mentioned it at the party. Any chance of our going out with you some time?'

'Certainly, whenever you like. I take her out most days.'

'We'll hold him to that, shall we, Caro? A forfeit for being so beastly to you just now.'

Caroline held her breath and Giles answered smoothly, 'I'd be glad to take you,

68

but as regards being beastly to Caroline, she's frequently beastly to me.'

Velma opened one eye. 'Really? In what way?'

There was a brief silence, fortunately broken by Simon, who said innocently, 'I told you before; she doesn't approve of the way he conducts his interviews.'

'Oh, that.' Velma lost interest. 'I shouldn't think you lose any sleep over it, do you, darling?'

Giles was saved from replying by someone calling, 'Hey, lunch is ready! Any takers over there?'

They made their way to the bar, where Madame Perrier and Yvette stood ready to serve the dishes chosen. There was *pissaladière*, a melting Provençal tart of onions, olives and anchovies, and salade Niçoise, with pale moist tuna nestling among the lettuce, and smoked sausage and ham, all accompanied by long loaves, a selection of cheeses and bowls of melons, pineapples, peaches and oranges.

They ate and swam and talked, and as the sun moved steadily round the pool they moved with it to avoid the shadows of the pine trees which began to point long fingers over the ground.

Caroline finished the book she was reading and sat up. The older people had gone back to the villa and only the youngest members of the

69

party were still dotted round the pool.

'So much for dinner down here, Simon,' Velma commented. 'Last time we did this it was July and the evenings were much warmer. It's still a bit early for that.' She was lying on her stomach, an arm flung possessively over Giles. As Caroline glanced at her, he removed it and stood up.

'One last swim, then, before we revert to shirts and sweaters.'

Velma scrambled to her feet. 'Race you to the far side!'

They dived together and set off across the water with long, even strokes.

'I do wish she wouldn't keep running after him,' Simon murmured.

'Do you think it's serious?'

'Lord knows. He's a cold sort of fish; I can't really make him out. He's always round here, but I think Grandmother's the attraction rather than Velma. They sit talking by the hour sometimes. She's very fond of him, I don't know why.'

Caroline was silent. She knew to her cost that the epithet 'cold fish' did not apply to Giles, but she was hardly in a position to say so.

Val Parkes and her fiancé came across to join them and as Giles and Velma returned, dripping, to their towels, the rest of them gathered their belongings and began to make their way up to the villa.

The evening was spent informally in the salon. One of the boys had a guitar and he sat on the floor strumming haunting old French airs. The plaintive laments had a lingering sadness which was reflected on the listening faces.

'Come on now, Steve, that's enough!' Val's father said at last. 'How about some happy songs we can all join in?'

So he changed to a selection of old favourites and the evening ended in a sing-song.

As she prepared for bed, Caroline reflected that she was satisfied with the day. She had been forced into Giles's company for the best part of it, and she had survived.

The following morning Humphrey Betts returned to his London office.

'It seems rather hard, knowing you're all still enjoying yourselves here!' Caroline commented to Simon as Gaston brought the car round to the door.

'He doesn't mind. He always says two to three weeks' holiday is as much as he can stand. I wonder if I'll feel the same next year, when I'm in the same position!'

Next year: was he supposing they'd be married by then? She said hurriedly, 'Hasn't Velma got a job?'

Simon snorted. 'Not so that you'd notice. She "helps out" in various friends' boutiques when the mood takes her—which it naturally doesn't as long as we're at the villa. I don't know how she gets away with it, but she seems to.'

'And I have the best of both worlds—two months here and actually being paid for it!'

Happily she thought of the satisfactory way that the book was going. She found she was looking forward to each new chapter as much as the eventual reader would: more so, since she could trace its beginnings in its author's head, the points at which she'd changed her mind slightly, brought one character to the fore, or faded out another.

For the next few days the work continued smoothly, but on the Thursday morning Berthe Perrier approached Caroline as she came downstairs to breakfast.

'Madame has asked me to extend her apologies, *mademoiselle*. Today she will stay in her room—she has the migraine. If your notes are up to date, she says you may amuse yourself.'

'Oh, I'm sorry!' Caroine exclaimed. 'Is there nothing I can do?'

'Alas no, *mademoiselle*. When the migraine comes, only darkness and quiet can help Madame. Sometimes it lasts two, three days. We must hope it will quickly pass.'

The day stretched emptily before her and having anticipated hours of stimulating work Caroline was reluctant simply to go down to the pool with another book. Simon and Velma were going out for the day with their mother and she didn't relish the prospect of her own company. She decided to go to St Luc. She had still not looked round the church or been in the museum.

Accordingly she went up to change out of her shorts and put on a blue and white gingham sundress which left back and shoulders bare. Then, with her camera and her outsize sunglasses, she went down the road to the bus stop.

It was a sizzling day but a strong wind was blowing—the *seruse*, she gathered from conversation on the bus. Certainly the faint haziness had been dispelled and the coastline round the bay was crystal clear.

She left the bus at the port and stood for several minutes looking about her. The row of boats, jostling cheek by jowl all round the harbour, fascinated her. At this early hour some of the decks were being hosed down, while on others entire families sat out enjoying breakfast in the full gaze of the passing throng. Flags and ports of all nationalities crowded together in haphazard camaraderie and she read the names painted on the hulls as she passed—Barbados, Mannheim, Viareggio, Bruxelles.

She walked slowly along the port, enjoying the bustle of activity that pervaded it. Across the road, café owners were wiping the overnight dew off tables and chairs and the

73

interminable racks of postcards were being set up on the pavement. Caroline paused to take several photographs before leaving the front to walk up one of the twisting cobbled roads towards the church.

It was too early for most of the shops to be open, but the *boulangeries* were doing a brisk trade and everyone Caroline met coming down the hill was armed with several long loaves. She stopped to look in the window. Honey bread, round bread, long and thin, not so long and fat, croissants and rolls—did any other nation eat as much bread as the French? The smell of it was too much for her. She went inside and bought a *'petit pain au chocolat'*, a small square of croissant pastry filled with bitter chocolate.

The assistant made some remark, Caroline eagerly replied, and since there was a temporary lull in customers, they chatted together for several minutes. It wasn't until she turned from the counter with her purchase that she saw Giles standing in the doorway.

'I must say, that was most impressive. Where did you learn to speak like that?'

'I lived in Normandy for a year.' She was taken completely by surprise at seeing him.

'Then you could be very useful to me, if you would. I bought a new battery for my razor the other day and the blasted thing won't work. I'm just on my way up to the shop and was wondering how to explain the trouble.' He paused. 'While I appreciate you're not normally disposed to do me favours, I really should be very grateful.'

'All right,' she said ungraciously, and looked away from his sardonic smile. He fell into step beside her as they went up the road, making their way round the huge terracotta pots of geraniums which seemed to be at every door.

When they reached their destination it took only a moment for Caroline to explain what was wrong with the battery. It was changed instantly, with a torrent of apologies.

'Simple when you know how,' Giles commented. 'Thank you.'

They started down the hill again, but at the first crossroads Caroline glanced to her right and saw a small market in progress at the foot of the alley. With an exclamation she darted towards it and after a moment Giles followed her. The end of the alley widened into a small courtyard and at the left-hand corner a flight of stone steps, bedecked with the usual tubs of flowers, led up to the open door of the house above. Alongside the staircase and in its shadow was the fish stall. Fish of all descriptions covered the counter—large whiting laid over huge slabs of ice, rubbery-looking eels, slender silver sardines, daurades, and shining heaps of black mussels.

In the centre of the courtyard were great buckets full of flowers carefully wrapped in cellophane, and alongside them the vegetable stall with huge bowls of green and black olives, woven plaits of garlic, purple aubergines, peppers, and tomatoes the size of apples.

Caroline stood stock-still, unmindful of the crowds pushing past her, feasting eyes and nose on the sights and smells that titillated the senses without even sampling them. 'Oh, I do love France!' she exclaimed impulsively.

'If you want to see a proper market you should go to the Place Marie-Sainte on Wednesdays and Saturdays. They have everything there—basketwork, figures carved out of olivewood, pottery—the lot.'

She turned reluctantly and they retraced their steps to the street leading down to the port. As they reached it, with one of the inevitable cafés alongside, Giles said, 'I'll buy you a drink by way of thanks. There's a free table there.'

'I haven't really—'

'Don't argue,' he said crisply. 'Sit down.'

She bit her lip, but unable to think of a suitable retort, did so. Without consulting her, Giles ordered two *cafés crème.* But the atmosphere around her made it difficult to remain out of harmony and by the time the drinks arrived she had relaxed, absorbing the ever-changing scene as people strolled past in twos and threes, and one or other of the boats moved out of harbour.

'You really do love it, don't you?' Giles commented.

'Oh yes, but I feel a bit cut off up at the villa. I much prefer to be part of it all, doing the shopping and feeling and sniffing the vegetables like the French housewives do, and bargaining in the market. And most of all I loved going out early in the morning when it was still a bit frosty—this was in Normandy, of course—for fresh bread and croissants, and then eating them with apricot jam and huge bowls of milky chocolate.'

She broke off suddenly and glanced across at him. He was watching her smilingly an odd expression in his eyes.

'Quite so,' he said drily as she came to an embarrassed halt. 'You'd forgotten who you were talking to, hadn't you? It must be difficult when you dislike someone so much—you can't let your guard slip for a second.'

'You don't understand,' she said miserably.

'Indeed I don't, since you refuse to explain, but it's your business after all. You're an intriguing girl, Caroline. Every time I see you, you display a new facet: meek little secretary, barb-tongued critic, passionate stranger, and now fluent linguist. What next, I wonder?'

'I think that's the full range,' she said tightly, swallowing the hot coffee.

They sat in silence, while around them the incessant laughing and chattering continued unabated. Suddenly Giles said abruptly, 'Has Simon asked you to marry him yet?' His eyes were narrowed, staring out across the bright water.

'Is it any business of yours?' she demanded heatedly.

'None, I'm just curious to know how your ploy is working.'

She felt as though he had slapped her face. As he'd said, she had allowed her guard to slip, albeit briefly, talking naturally to him for the first time. And then, out of the blue, this.

'You haven't a very high opinion of me, have you?' she asked in a low voice.

'On the contrary. As I just said, I have the greatest admiration for your versatility. You must remember always to display the right face to Simon, though. He might become bewildered by the variety. "Will the real Caroline Cain please stand up?" Keep trying, my dear, you're sure to land him in the end.'

'Since you're so interested,' she flashed, 'he *has* asked me to marry him!' She stopped, appalled, aware of having been stampeded into the admission which as yet was entirely between Simon and herself.

'Ah!' said Giles. 'Congratulations.'

She said dully, 'I shouldn't have told you. No one knows yet.'

'I shall be the soul of discretion.'

Caroline stood up abruptly, almost upsetting the tray of the waiter who was coming up behind her.

'You are without doubt the most hateful man I've ever met!'

He raised an eyebrow. 'Do I gather you're leaving?'

She turned and started to thread her way through the chairs. Behind her she heard him drop some coins on the table and come after her. She quickened her pace and in her haste looked right instead of left as she stepped off the kerb. Giles's hand caught her arm, pulling her violently back, and even as she fought to free herself a car whizzed past only inches away.

'Would you rather go under a car than have me touch you?' he demanded harshly, and added under his breath, 'I almost believe you would!'

She stood trembling, looking up into his hard face.

'You must know you're in no danger of my—attacking you again,' he went on more levelly. 'I know who you are this time. So, having been reassured on that point, would you like a lift back?'

'No. Thank you.'

'You'd prefer to walk?'

'If necessary, but I'm not going back yet.'

'No work today?'

'No. Mrs Stevens has a migraine.'

'Poor Adeline, she's plagued with those things.' He hesitated. 'Thanks for your help with the battery.'

'It was a pleasure,' she said acidly.

'I realise I could have been more cordial. I'd

79

intended to be, but unfortunately you bring out the worst in me.'

'I had noticed.'

He smiled slightly. 'You're sure about the lift?'

'Yes, thank you. Goodbye.' And she swung away from him, up the hill again. This time, without really thinking, she kept heading to the left, past shaded little squares with huge plane trees in the centre of them, past old fountains decorated with gargoyle heads, past the church she had intended to look over but now found herself in no mood for. On the pavements artists had set up easels at strategic points and each ancient flight of stone steps, each tilting wall covered with flowers, was having its replica faithfully reproduced on canvas.

Still Caroline kept climbing, her mind churning with furious resentment. How had he described her? 'Barb-tongued critic, passionate stranger.' She would not have recognised either as a description of herself, but she supposed he was right on both counts. She paused to survey the large stone trough which formed the communal wash-house, and beyond it the field of fluttering washing drying in the breezy sunshine. A cat blinked sleepily at her from a worn doorstep, an old woman, in perennial black, sat crocheting in the shade.

It was almost noon now, the sun high in the sky. The village was dropping away behind her

80

as she came out on the scrubby hillside above. Here, all was silence, the air heavily perfumed with the scent of pines and alive with the whirring of crickets. Cacti also grew profusely, round and flat like table-tennis bats, tall and spiky with brilliant red flowers, and date palms with their strange corky trunks. Still above her loomed the grey ruins of the ancient citadel which had defended St Luc through the long centuries: against Moslem pirates, Germanic invasions, and the wars of the Middle Ages and Renaissance.

She turned and caught her breath at the view spread before her. Immediately below lay the village, a higgledy-piggledy nest of terracotta roofs, cream, pink and ochre walls, blue and white shutters, and in the centre, high above the rest, the old clock-tower of the church. At the near end of the port she could see the stout stone buttress with the steps leading up from the beach, where she had climbed with Simon. Beyond the stone outcrop the low white breakwater swept round to protect the port of St Luc, filled with its dazzling white boats, yachts with high masts raking the sky, cabin cruisers, sleek and streamlined. Sky and water were an unbelievable blue and as she watched a speedboat cut its way out beyond the bay, churning the water behind it in a creamy wake.

Caroline sat down, hugging her knees and letting her eyes move slowly over the wealth spread before her. And a line from a hymn came into her mind: 'Where every prospect pleases, and only man is vile.'

'Man,' she said aloud grimly 'being the operative word!'

She realised she was hungry and, forsaking her perch, started down the hill, stopping at a kiosk to buy the local *pan bagnat*—in effect a salad roll—which she ate appreciatively as she walked.

Down on the front again, she stopped to buy two warm ripe peaches as a get-well gift for Mrs Stevens, and then wended her way down the steps on to the beach. At the water's edge a group of fishermen were engaged in mending their nets and farther out on the rocks the inevitable sunbathers spread out limbs of varying colours. There was a strong smell of fish and salt and seaweed.

It was a much quicker way home along the beach than the tortuous road which the bus had to take. In a short while she passed the steps leading to Giles's villa and then, a little farther on, climbed their own.

She would enquire how Adeline was, present her with the peaches if she happened to be awake, and then pay her postponed visit to the pool. She felt hot and sticky after walking in the sun. She went straight upstairs therefore, and paused at the door to her employer's room. A low murmur of voices reached her. The family must have returned from their day out, she thought with a spurt of gladness, having had enough of her own company. She tapped on the door and pushed it open, but to her dismay it was Giles who was sitting at the bedside. He rose to his feet, eyes mocking her.

Ignoring him, Caroline turned to the woman sitting up in bed. 'I came to ask how you were.'

'Much better, my dear, as you see. I've just ordered some tea. Call down to Berthe, and ask her to put another cup and saucer on the tray.'

Useless to protest; Adeline would not take kindly to her orders being questioned. Miserably Caroline did as she was told. It seemed there was no escape from Giles Guthrie these days.

'I brought you a couple of peaches,' she said on her return, laying them on the counterpane.

'How very sweet of you, dear. Thank you so much. Did you enjoy your unexpected free day?'

Caroline was aware of Giles's amused attention as he waited for her reply. She said indirectly, 'I climbed the hill towards the citadel. There's a magnificent view from up there.'

'And there it is!' Adeline flung out her arm with a flourish, and following its direction, Caroline saw that the painting on the far wall was indeed the scene she had enjoyed from the top of the hill.

Mrs Stevens turned back to Giles. 'I'm sorry, I've interrupted you. You were telling me about the series of articles you're planning.'

He hesitated. 'I don't suppose Caroline would be interested in hearing all the details.'

'*I* should be interested,' Adeline said sharply, 'and I imagine Caroline would too. She's an intelligent girl, you know. I don't employ fools.'

'I'm sure you don't,' he said gravely.

She glanced at him with narrowed eyes. 'Don't humour me, Giles. I never allow people to humour me.'

He laughed suddenly. 'I wouldn't be so presumptuous! Well, as you know, I felt I could only justify a prolonged stay here if I turned it to good account, so basically the series is to be on all things French: the ways of life in the Midi, the part that progress in agriculture and education has played in furthering the decay of the ancient villages; Provençal architecture, industry, politics—I could go on indefinitely.'

'You would have to be extremely knowledgeable!'

'The facts are easily obtained. The challenge will be putting together the series to make an informed and, one hopes, interesting whole.'

A tap on the door heralded Madame Perrier

with the tray. Caroline jumped up to help her and, when she left the room, poured out the tea at Adeline's request.

'This climate certainly seems to agree with you,' the elderly woman remarked, her approving eyes moving over the girl's glowing, bronzed skin. 'You look as rosy and succulent as those peaches, doesn't she, Giles?'

'Indeed she does,' Giles murmured, his eyes on Caroline's flushed cheeks.

'It does my heart good to see the change in her. She had a bad time last winter, but it's behind her now. Right, child?'

'Yes, Mrs Stevens.' Except for the constant reminder which, unknown to either of them, Giles kept providing.

She drank her tea dutifully, refilled Mrs Stevens' cup and also Giles's, without once meeting his eye. Only then did she feel free to make her escape.

'Is there anything else I can get you, Mrs Stevens?'

'No, my dear, I have everything I need, thank you. All being well, I'll be back at work in the morning.'

'Good. Then if you'll excuse me I think I'll have a swim. I'm so glad you're feeling better.' And, thankfully, she left them. Had her employer noticed any coolness between herself and Giles? If so, she had given no sign of it.

Determinedly dismissing him from her mind, she went to collect her swimming things.

CHAPTER FIVE

The next few days passed uneventfully. To make up for the lost day of her migraine, Adeline seemed intent on covering as much ground as possible, and Caroline's free afternoons were for the most part spent either by the pool or on the beach with Simon. Yet despite the amount of time they were together, she was uncomfortably aware of a feeling of restraint between them.

That she wasn't the only one to notice it was brought home to her early one evening as, ready for the dinner party Adeline was giving, she leaned out of her bedroom window looking at the still-green garden with the first of the evening shadows falling across it. She was vaguely aware of voices in the salon below, but the lintel over the patio doors muted them. Only when the speakers moved out on to the terrace immediately below the window did they identify themselves as Giles and Velma.

Caroline drew back inside and was about to move away when her own name arrested her attention. It was Giles who was speaking.

'I must admit she's not the type I'd have expected him to go for.'

'But that's the whole point—he didn't! You'd never believe she's the same girl we met in London! In my opinion he's discovering he's bitten off more than he can chew. Poor Simon! The timid little kitten he befriended has grown into a tiger!'

Caroline moved swiftly back, her breath coming fast. Was it true? Was Simon regretting the closeness which still held them together? Echoes of previous conversations came disturbingly to mind. Giles by the pool: 'I should have thought you'd be too much for him to handle.' Simon himself: 'Now that you're self-confident again you don't seem to need me as you did.'

And again: 'You seemed lovelier to me in London, when you were so pale and desperate.'

Thoughtfully smoothing her hands over the figure-hugging dress of coffee lace, she remembered the severe skirts and blouses she'd worn when she first met Simon—remembered, too, his annoyance when the boys had whistled after her in St Luc. Didn't he *want* to be proud of her? she asked herself impatiently. Did her regained assurance present him with some kind of threat?

Downstairs the bell clanged through the house announcing the arrival of more dinner guests and Caroline went down to join them. There were to be six that evening and Adeline had given her a quick run-down of them: Marguerite Collière, a famous star of the French screen during the 'forties, and her latest young lover—Adeline was not sure of his name: Jeremy Tait, the renowned British author—'a bit odd, my dear, but a charming man for all that'—Paul and Felicity Grant, an American couple with a string of West End plays to their credit, and François Lebrun, a restaurateur who had known the family for years. 'And of course,' Adeline had added smilingly, 'Giles, our own resident celebrity, who can hold his own with the best of them. I tend to forget he isn't family.'

It was not a point Caroline was likely to overlook.

During drinks on the terrace she made little contribution to the conversation, content to sit back and feast her ears and eyes on the famous people congregating so casually about her. Marguerite Collière's face was a mask, a doll-like arrangement of features with so many face-lifts behind them that all expression had been erased like the wiping clean of a blackboard. Brows finely arched, nostrils aristocratically pinched, gilded hair immaculate, only the eyes were alive and, fearful and possessive, they seldom left the youth on whose arm she had arrived. How *could* he? Caroline thought shudderingly, her own eyes going to the boy, roughly the same age as herself, with his lithe young body and melting brown eyes.

The Grants she liked immediately. They were friendly and unaffected, seemingly as awed by their illustrious companions as was

Caroline herself. For the rest, Jeremy Tait was about seventy, large and pompous, and François Lebrun in his fifties, smooth, dapper, and almost excessively French. Caroline noted that Lydia Betts, in the absence of her husband, had appropriated him for the evening. And of course there was Giles, in navy blazer and white trousers, impossibly tanned and suave and at ease.

Caroline looked quickly away, wondering rather nervously whom she would be placed beside at dinner. It transpired she was between Lebrun and Paul Grant, and she relaxed, automatically registering that Giles was at the far end of the table from her.

During the course of the meal the conversation turned, not unexpectedly, to the French cinema, and as always in such circumstances it was not long before someone mentioned the name of the great director Henri Duval. Remembering the number of times she had queued to see his films, Caroline was enthralled to realise that some of these people actually knew him.

'And of course,' Marguerite Collière was saying, 'his greatest triumph to date was *La Petite amie*, which Michel produced.'

'But surely, *madame*,' Caroline broke in, too interested in the conversation to judge whether her intervention was welcome—'it was Marcel Juste who produced *La Petite amie*?' As every pair of eyes at the table swivelled in her direction, she murmured in confusion, *'Pardon, madame, je m'excuse.'*

'Mademoiselle knows the works of Duval?' Animations at last flickered on the waxen features of Marguerite Collière. 'And she also speaks French?'

'I—yes,' Caroline confessed on both counts. 'I've seen all his films. I think he's—quite fabulous.'

'But this is fantastic!' exclaimed François Lebrun, clapping his hands. 'In this so quiet *demoiselle* we have an expert on the French cinema!'

To her embarrassment Caroline found herself the centre of attention, and when the meal was over, Madame Collière bore down on her and swept her off into a corner of the room with a flood of French. Caroline responded as best she could, aware of pity for this woman who could not accept that she was growing old, who was pathetically eager to talk about the films of her youth which to Caroline were classics of an age before she was born.

'Of course, Henri came much later,' Marguerite admitted with disarming candour. He is still a relatively young man and has many years yet ahead of him. He could well become the greatest director France has ever known. He has a villa not too far from here at Ste Emmanuelle.'

The boy Raoul Puy hovered near them, though his large seductive eyes rested more frequently on Caroline than on his *patronn.* And after a while Giles too drew up a chair. Marguerite broke off in mid-sentence.

'Please carry on,' he said quickly. 'You seemed so engrossed in your conversation I wondered if I might listen too.'

She laughed lightly. 'It would do you little good, *mon cher,* since we were speaking in French.' She glanced at Caroline. 'In truth, I'd forgotten you were English, *mademoiselle,* you speak so perfectly. But now we must revert to your own tongue for the sake of this so English gentleman!'

'I beg your pardon,' Giles said wryly. 'Stupid of me—I hadn't realised—'

'No matter.' Marguerite raised her hand. 'We are both, I believe, proficient in either language. But the knowledge of this young lady, not only of French but of the works of Duval, that I find astonishing.'

'There are many things about Caroline that are astonishing,' Giles said quietly, but when she glanced at him questioningly his eyes were on the French woman.

'*Franchement?* How intriguing! Now tell me, Giles, what is it that interests you about Duval?'

'He's an essential part of twentieth-century French culture,' Giles replied. 'There aren't too many people one can describe in that way.'

'Well said, my friend. That. pleases me—a happy choice of phrase.'

Raoul Puy came closer and murmured something in Marguerite's ear. She reached up almost absent-mindedly, ruffling his hair as one would fondle a puppy's ears. That's what he was Caroline thought pityingly, a lapdog trained to give affection in return for food and shelter. It was grotesque to see the two faces so close together, Madame old enough to be his grandmother.

Marguerite rose to her feet, murmured her excuses, and moved away with the young man's arm round her tightly corseted waist. Caroline watched them go, then turned reluctantly back to Giles.

'That was a very enigmatic expression on your face,' he said quietly. 'What exactly were you thinking?'

'How sad it would be, to have to try to buy love,' she answered, and saw that she had surprised him.

'You don't think it's possible?'

'It depends on your definition of love.'

'And what is yours?'

She looked at him consideringly. 'Quite different from yours, I don't doubt.'

'Implying that mine would be found wanting. I hoped for once we might manage a reasonably intelligent conversation, but your prejudices always get in the way.'

Velma came up behind him, slid her long arms round his neck and rested her cheek on the top of his head. 'I'm getting restive, love,' she murmured, loud enough for Caroline to hear. 'Let's go out for a breath of air.'

'In a moment,' he replied dismissively. Over his head, Velma's eyes met Caroline's.

'You certainly distinguished yourself,' she remarked with an edge to her voice. 'I held my breath when you interrupted La Collière, but since you knew what you were talking about, she forgave you.'

'She did more than that,' Giles put in. 'She was quite overwhelmed by Caroline's prowess.'

'Aren't we all?' Velma murmured spitefully.

'Can one buy love, Velma?'

'Lord, what a poser! What brought that on?'

'Marguerite and the boy.'

'I shouldn't call that love. Lying with him in the dark, she can pretend she's forty years younger, that's all.'

Caroline stood up abruptly and moved away. It was obvious that Velma's heartless complacency had blinded her to the tragedy in the situation. Poor Marguerite, and poor Raoul. Their sordid relationship served only to show up the inadequacies in each of them, and they were more to be pitied than condemned.

The following afternoon when as usual Caroline returned to the study at four o'clock, it was to find Giles sitting with Adeline. She hesitated in the doorway, but her employer beckoned her.

'Come in, my dear, and sit down. Giles has a proposition and I'd like to know how you feel

93

about it.'

Warily Caroline's eyes went from her face to his. 'What kind of proposition?'

'Tell her, Giles.'

'I mentioned the other day these articles I'm writing on various aspects of French life. On the arts side, I'd already made a list of people I'd like to interview, and Henri Duval was among them. It emerged last night that he's staying at his villa in Ste Emmanuelle. If I can persuade him to see me, I was wondering if you'd care to come along and act as my interpreter? He doesn't speak English.'

Caroline stared at him, feeling herself go hot.

'Well, child? You seemed very interested in his work.'

'Giles knows I don't approve of his interviewing methods.'

'Ye gods! You imagine I could reduce the great Duval to a quivering wreck? Anyway, if you're there to protect him, you could tone down the more "degrading" questions.'

'Mrs Stevens, I'm here as your secretary. I don't—'

'Giles respects that, which is why he came to me in the first place to ask my permission. Naturally if you'd prefer not to go, you've only to say so. I don't doubt he could hire an official interpreter, but I thought it might be a break for you. It would be a chance to see a different part of Provence and meet a man you

94

so obviously admire.'

And it would, of course. She could never have imagined, sitting entranced in those dark cinemas, that she would one day have the chance to meet Duval—and turn it down!

Still she hesitated. 'What about your book?'

'It would only mean missing one day, and I could use the tape if invention got the better of me.'

Unwillingly Caroline turned back to Giles. 'You haven't actually made an appointment?'

'Not yet. He might not agree to see me. On the other hand, like all great men he's not without his share of vanity, and it would be excellent publicity.'

'Well?' Adeline prompted. 'What do you think?'

'All right.' Caroline reached a decision. 'Provided it won't inconvenience you, I don't mind going.'

'Kind of you,' Giles said tightly. He turned to Adeline. 'I'll try to phone him this evening and let you know what he says.'

The door closed behind him, and Adeline looked thoughtfully at her secretary's flushed cheeks. 'There's something between you and Giles, isn't there? Am I being unnecessarily dense?'

'We don't like each other, that's all,' Caroline replied with lowered eyes.

'I see,' Adeline said after a moment. There was a brief pause. 'Well, we'll put the matter aside until he comes back to us. In the meantime, have you your notebook?'

His telephone call came just before dinner. Adeline took it in the study, then, summoning Caroline, left her to speak to him.

'One slight problem.' Giles's voice was clipped. "The only free time he has is Friday evening. The interview will probably go on fairly late and Ste Emmanuelle is a good two hours' drive from here. It will mean staying away overnight.'

Caroline swallowed. 'You told Mrs Stevens?'

'Yes. It's all right with her, especially since you're free on Saturdays. And since I shall of course be paying for your services, you'll earn yourself a nice little bonus, which should take away some of the bad taste. So, if you're still prepared to come, I'll call for you after lunch on Friday.'

'Very well,' she said quietly, and dropped the receiver back on its rest.

Adeline reappeared in the doorway. 'All right?'

'I suppose so,' said Caroline.

Throughout Wednesday and Thursday Caroline swung continuously between resigning herself to the arrangement and deciding to phone and cancel it. But it was worth a lot to meet Henri Duval, and when Giles drove up in his Peugeot she was waiting with notebooks and her overnight bag.

He got out of the car, glanced at her set face, and put her case in the boot. 'Is Adeline resting?'

'Yes.'

'We might as well go, then.'

They swooped down the villa drive and out on to Avenue Pascal, with its eucalyptus trees and high, wild rhododendrons. Giles turned right and swung up the slight hill to the main St Luc road, past the bus stop where Caroline had so often waited. The road was almost deserted since it was the two-hour lunch break and only a few tourists were about. On either side palms and pine trees intermingled in botanical confusion.

Giles glanced at her. 'I banked on your interest in Duval outweighing your dislike of me.'

'Very astute of you.'

'You can relax, you know. I don't bite—often.'

He was wearing sunglasses and she couldn't see his expression. The idea that she would be spending the best part of the next twenty-four hours in his company filled her with a mixture of disquiet and a sick excitement she made no attempt to define.

They were coming down the hill into St Luc. On either side houses lined the road, four-square like a child's drawing, each with its tall narrow windows shuttered against the sun and its ludicrously shallow roof, like a too-small

97

hat perched on its head. Then they were through the village and coming up the hill on the far side. Giles drove fast and competently, his brown hands firm on the wheel. Caroline was acutely aware of the smell of him, compounded of tobacco and after-shave and clean linen. She thought in a panic: I shouldn't have come!

His voice broke into her thoughts. 'Adeline said the other day you'd had a rough time. What happened?'

Caroline tasted the blood on her tongue. 'My father died.'

'I'm sorry. Have you no other close relations?'

'None of any kind.'

'That is hard. And you hadn't a job either, till you found this one?'

'I had one lined up, but it was dependent on getting my degree.'

'Couldn't you have stayed on at university?'

'Possibly. I don't know. I wasn't thinking straight at the time.' Her voice shook. 'Can we change the subject?'

He said more gently, 'Adeline's very fond of you.'

'It's mutual.'

'Yes, I know. Caroline—'

'Yes?'

'Never mind.' He put his foot down and the car shot forward. They had left the coastline and started to climb into the mountains that lay so close behind. The white road, dazzling in the sun, twisted its way through deeply wooded crevasses whose sheer heights rose directly from the road. Trees, plants and shrubs crowded together in colourful and almost indecent fecundity, silver-grey olives contrasting with dark, wind-bent conifers, the soft apple-green of new ferns among ramrod sticks of bamboo. Once in a while they flashed past a wayside shrine, with its ochre stone and vivid splash of flowers. There were occasional glimpses of the steeply-tiled roofs of a distant village, and warning notices by the roadside implored passers-by *'Pensez à la forêt'*, a poignant reminder of the fires which could gain so swift and fatal a hold.

'Do you know anything about the place where we're going?' asked Giles.

She shook her head.

'It's one of the famous "perched villages". You find them all over the place down here, built right at the top of a steep hill, seeming part of the actual rock. Often you have to park at the bottom and go up on foot.'

'What was the point of them?' she asked.

'They were natural fortresses, very necessary in those unsettled days. Most of them have ramparts and battlements, sometimes a château. A lot of them are almost abandoned now.'

The road was still climbing and on their right the slopes fell steeply away so that they were able to look down on the plump green cushions of parasol pines, the contrasting shades of beech, oak and chestnut.

'There's some kind of ruin up there,' Caroline said suddenly, pointing to her left. 'I wonder what it is.'

'Would you like to have a look? We've plenty of time in hand.' He pulled the car off the road and came to a halt. Above them the hill rose less steeply, covered in lavender bushes whose sweet perfume stole down the slopes towards them. At the top, a grey stone outline was stencilled against the brazen blue of the sky.

Caroline said doubtfully, 'It looks a long way up.'

'Distances are deceptive,' Giles replied decisively. 'It won't take us more than fifteen minutes to reach it, and I imagine the view from up there will be well worth the effort. What kind of shoes are you wearing?'

She glanced down at her sandals. 'Not exactly climbing boots!'

'They'll be a bit slippery, but you can hang on to me.' And, at her quick glance, 'Or would you prefer to break your neck?'

She opened the car door and climbed out, standing gazing around her as Giles locked the doors.

'Come on,' he said briskly. 'And like it or not, I'd advise you to take my hand.'

Meekly she put her small hand into his and

felt it close round her fingers. Keeping her eyes firmly on the ground, she set off, slightly behind him, putting her feet in the footholds he found for her. The sun beat down on their backs and they climbed in silence. The under-growth, scree and small rocks, was treacherously slippery and several times Caroline would have fallen had not Giles's hand held her firmly upright. Within a few yards of their goal the slope eased and they were almost on level ground. He did not, however, release her hand, and she dared make no movement of withdrawal. Side by side they came at last to the crumbling ruin which had attracted their attention. Inside its broken walls nettles grew rampant, but the smell of wild herbs—thyme and rosemary mingling with the lavender—rose in waves in the hot air.

They turned to look back the way they had come and Caroline caught her breath. Beneath them the ground fell away to the road and the small blue roof of the Peugeot, glinting like a toy far below. On the other side of it were wooden slopes interspersed with the roofs of isolated houses, while above and beyond them fold after fold of hills stretched away into the distance. Heat lay over everything, blurring outlines into a shimmering softness, and in all the wide panorama there was no sign of a living thing, though invisible crickets chirruped persistently all around them.

Caroline became aware of Giles's stillness at her side and the fact that her hand was still in his. It seemed safer to disengage it, and this she did.

'Well, was it worth the climb?' he asked.

'It's magnificent, isn't it? I wonder what you can see from the other side of the ruin.'

'Do you want to walk round and have a look?'

'It'd be quicker to climb up and look through that hole.'

She scrambled, slipping and sliding, across the uneven ground between the walls and pulled herself up by the crumbling rock of the ancient window embrasure. The drop to the ground on the far side was six feet or so, and beyond a narrow shelf of grass the ground fell away to another breathtaking vista. She turned, balanced on her ledge, to see Giles standing where she had left him.

'I've an aversion to nettles. You were lucky to escape unscathed. If the view's worth seeing I'll make my way round. Is it?'

'Yes, it's glorious. You can just catch a glimpse of the sea between two hills.'

'I'm on my way.'

She turned back to the blues and greens spread out before her and a moment later he came round the jutting rock on her right and stood below her, gazing as she had at the panorama.

'That patch of sea is just beyond St Luc.

We've come quite a long way, as you can see.'
He turned and looked up at her. 'Are you
coming down, or do you intend to roost up
there indefinitely?'

She looked doubtfully at the considerable
distance between herself and the ground. 'I
think I'd better go back the way I came.'

'I shouldn't advise it. It's harder going
downhill and the nettles are lying in wait.
Jump down this side. It's not too far and I'll
catch you.'

'The edge of the cliff looks uncomfortably
close,' she said uneasily.

'I doubt if your weight would knock me off
balance. Anyway, there's a good ten feet
behind me. Come on—jump!'

Any idea of letting herself down more
gently disintegrated with the stone her
searching foot had located. Since she'd no
choice she launched herself off her perch, and
as she landed Giles's arms came firmly round
her. Even so she stumbled against him, heard
his indrawn breath and his unsteady comment:
'You're an enthusiastic jumper, I must say!'

He held her slightly away from him, eyes
raking her face, noting her parted lips, her
rapid breathing not entirely explainable by her
leap to the ground. And he said very softly,
'Oh, Caroline!'

Helplessly she felt herself pulled close
again, the rigidity of his body pressing against
her, his open mouth moving over her ears, her

hair. With every last ounce of willpower she pushed herself away before his mouth found hers.

For a moment they stood facing each other, breathing quickly, eyeing each other warily. Then she forced herself to say, 'We'd better go down.'

'As you say. I'll go first.'

No suggestion this time of taking her hand, and she would have died sooner than suggest it. Giles would have broken her fall had she slipped, but the thought of such close contact with him was sufficient for her to maintain an almost miraculous balance all the way down.

'Quite the mountain goat, aren't you?' he said acidly as they reached the safety of the car. Yet his tone had been quite different up on the hill, she remembered as the car leapt back on to the road and set off again. Something in his voice as he said 'Oh, Caroline!' had started her blood racing and her stomach churning, while memories of that night on the terrace, which she thought she had managed to obliterate, came flooding back again. Yet that voice, deep and tender, was the one that had once said with such urbane cruelty: 'I put it to you, Mr Cain—'

She clenched her hands in her lap, fighting to hold back tears of shame—regret—frustration. Beside her Giles drove rapidly, expertly manoeuvring the twisting road. A surreptitious glance at his face showed his mouth to be hard and set. As before, the sunglasses hid his eyes.

The road had dropped now to a valley and some miles ahead of them, rising abruptly from the level plain, jutted the precipitous rock to which, for countless centuries, the old houses of Ste Emmanuelle had precariously clung.

Since someone had to break the silence, Caroline said tentatively, 'Does Monsieur Duval live actually in the village?'

'Yes.'

Very well, if he was determined not to speak, she too would keep quiet. Minutes later as they came up under the hill, Giles said curtly, 'We can drive up part of the way, it seems.'

In fact the parking area, railed off from the steep drop below, was immediately opposite the hotel. Giles turned into it and switched off the engine. Without looking at her he took her case and his own valise out of the boot and set off across the palm-shaded road to the sleepy-looking hotel. Caroline followed at a distance, resenting his off handedness but knowing her reaction on the hillside to be the cause of it. Giles Guthrie was obviously not used to having his advances repelled.

The clerk behind the desk was obtusely refusing to understand Giles's questions. As he scrawled his name in the register he said tersely, 'Find out what time they serve dinner

105

till, will you? We don't want to get back and find the kitchens closed.'

'That doesn't happen in France.'

'I'm not interested in generalities. See how late we can eat.'

Rapidly Caroline did so and the lazy clerk straightened, eyeing her with more interest.

'As I said,' Caroline reported briefly, 'at any time we like.'

'Good, because I certainly couldn't eat beforehand. It's four-thirty now and the interview isn't till seven. Please be down here in the foyer at six forty-five.'

'Yes, sir.'

He looked at her suspiciously, but she met his gaze with bland innocence. The clerk picked up the two cases and with a muttered request to Caroline, moved towards the lift. She followed him, and after a moment's hesitation Giles came after them. They rode up to the third floor in silence. It was, she felt, going to be a taxing twenty-four hours.

CHAPTER SIX

As the door closed behind the clerk Caroline looked round the room allotted to her. A large double bed, demurely covered in white candlewick, a rickety wardrobe and a small bathroom to one side. Behind the shutters the sunlight beat down, patterning the tiled floor with golden bars. Two and a half hours. She had no intention of staying here all that time.

She took the dress she had brought for the interview out of the case, shook it and hung it in the wardrobe. Then, armed with her camera, she let herself quietly out of her room, made her way downstairs and out into the baking street. Opposite her, beyond the rail of the car-park, lay the plain they had crossed to reach here, massive and glimmering in the heat.

A twisting road led upwards from the square where she stood, and Caroline accepted its invitation. Everywhere there were flowers—gigantic lilies, a searing orange against their dark green spikes, honeysuckle, purple convolvulus—all so much larger and more prolific than she had always considered the norm. The houses which lined the street opened directly off the pavement, their open doorways shielded by bead curtains, their shuttered windows protected by intricately wrought ironwork. And at each doorway stood the invariable terracotta pots, filled with succulents, ferns and hydrangeas. From one of the open windows drifted the essentially French sound of an accordion.

At the top of the street she came upon another square, its low walls decorated with pots of cacti. Vines climbed over doorways and a large elm spread a welcome shade over a

107

little white table and chairs. Fuchsias and wisteria spilled over the worn stone and there was a pungent smell of roasting coffee.

Driven by some urge she had not stopped to examine, Caroline continued her climb, finally emerging below the ramparts of the old fortified town. Here warning notices outlined the dangerous condition of the ruins, absolving the authorities from any liability for injury. And if she climbed up there, Giles would not be waiting to catch her.

She turned away abruptly and started to make her way down, following a different road this time, from which flights of steps led up to doors at the first floor level and archways complete with windows spanned the narrow space between the sides of the street. Shops were opening again after their long siesta and in the window of the charcuterie covers were being removed from huge rounds of stuffed roast veal, highly seasoned sausages and slices of pie.

Oh, Caroline! Giles had said. Suppose she had not moved away, allowed the embrace to continue. What then? A tide of weakness swamped her and she put out a hand to steady herself. Up there on the steep hillside they had been completely alone and there was no dark garden in which she could have run to hide. There was a yearning ache inside her, an acknowledgement that she almost wished he had insisted despite her withdrawal.

The realisation took her by surprise and she hurriedly fitted it into an acceptable perspective. Admittedly he had aroused her, that evening at the villa and to a lesser extent on the hill: but only because Simon's kisses were so tame and watered-down. It was Giles's masculinity, his ruthless, demanding virility that she responded to. The person behind the body, offhand, calculating, cruel, she was still able to detest.

At the foot of the street she had a moment's anxiety that she had lost her way, but to her relief she saw, a few levels below her, the parking space with the blue Peugeot, and minutes later she reached the hotel and her room. She went straight to the bathroom and treated herself to an invigorating shower, gradually turning the tap until ice-cold needles stung her body to a rosy glow.

The dress she had brought with her was a soft cotton in maize yellow, with tiny buttons from low neckline to waist. The high-heeled sandals complemented her slender brown legs and round her neck she fastened the gold chain she always wore.

'Eh bien, monsieur le directeur!' she thought to herself. *'Je suis prête.'*

A tap on the door spun her round, and Giles's voice called, 'Caroline—are you there?'

She glanced at her watch in surprise. It was only six-thirty. She opened the door, catching a fleeting look of relief on his face.

'Where have you been?' he demanded.

'Out. Why?'

'I came back as soon as I'd unpacked. I couldn't think where you were.'

'You wondered if I'd gone straight home?'

He met her eyes. 'It was on the cards.'

'Yes,' she returned calmly, surprising herself, 'after your behaviour, I suppose it was.'

She'd been referring to his abruptness on their arrival, and realised too late that his own mind had gone back to the confrontation on the hill. Colour swept up her face, and to hide it she turned away and pretended to sort out the things in her handbag.

'Why were you looking for me?' she asked.

'To apologise for said behaviour. We'll have to present a united front to Duval, so I thought we'd better smooth things over.'

'Otherwise, of course, you wouldn't have bothered.'

'Let's not indulge in speculation. I do apologise and I hope you'll accept it. Now, if you spare a few minutes I want to discuss our plan of campaign. He's a difficult man, I'm told, and we'll need to get behind his reserve. You can butter him up to start with, by raving over his films.'

'Thanks.'

'Then we want to get him reminiscing— moments of temperament with the stars, his relationship with the studio bosses—you know

110

the kind of thing. And, of course, his plans for the future. You have notebooks with you, I presume?'

'Naturally.'

'I brought a cassette recorder in case you miss anything.'

'I shouldn't, since I'll be using French shorthand.'

'*French* shorthand?' he echoed.

'Well, of course. English phonetics would be useless.'

'You'll take down what he says in French?'

She looked at him in exasperation. 'You don't seem to have given this much thought. I could hardly take the time to translate it as he's actually speaking. We'd be there all night.'

'Of course. It simply didn't occur to me. So we discover yet another of your accomplishments. You're quite a girl, aren't you?'

'I shouldn't have agreed to come if I hadn't been sure I could cope,' she shrugged.

'With me or Duval?'

'Both of you!'

Giles smiled slightly. 'All right, Joan of Arc, let's go.'

The intensity had left the sun, which now hung low over the valley. Giles's hand was lightly under her elbow and she schooled her leaping pulses to ignore his touch.

'Where did your exploration take you this afternoon?' he asked.

111

'Up to the top of the village, by the ramparts.'

'You're a great one for heights, aren't you?'

'I've an ambitious nature,' she answered lightly.

'So I've noticed.'

'Which does not,' she added calmly, 'include marrying for money, before you bring that up again.'

She felt his quick glance, but all he said was: 'Here we are. Let's hope we get something worth while.'

A high, honey-coloured wall surrounded the villa. In the middle of it was an equally high gate, complete with a bell. Giles pressed it, a disembodied voice asked their business, and a moment later a servant came to admit them. They were led not into the house but round the corner on to a wide, shady patio looking out across the valley. A fountain played gently in one corner and a stone statue peered coyly round some oleanders. From the depths of a canvas chair, glass in hand, Henri Duval rose to greet them.

He was a tall, thin man in his early forties, with cavernous cheeks, a wide, high forehead and a disenchanted look in his eyes. He greeted them formally and at a sign from Giles, Caroline explained her rôle. Duval nodded, complimented her briefly on her fluency, and indicated the chairs round the white iron table. Drinks were brought

112

for them.

'This must be boring for you, *mademoiselle,* to be pressed into interviewing an obscure film director?'

Giles had said great men had their vanity, but there was no need for insincere flattery. 'On the contrary, *monsieur,* it's a great privilege to meet you. I've admired your work for as long as I can remember.'

He raised an eyebrow, not entirely convinced. 'And which of my films did you prefer?' he asked softly. A pitfall indeed, if she had been bluffing. Instead, she launched enthusiastically into detailed comparisons of at least four, mentioning specific scenes and snatches of dialogue which had particularly impressed her. By this time Henri Duval was sitting forward, his eyes intent on her face, and when she finally came to a halt his face broke into a smile which completely transformed it, revealing him, surprisingly, as a most attractive man.

He turned charmingly to Giles. 'Forgive me, *monsieur.* Instead of your interviewing me, I am questioning your secretary. I am, of course, at your disposal.'

When Caroline translated Giles smiled and made a deprecating gesture, but his eyes, too, were on her animated face, his attention on the lilting fluency with which she spoke.

Around them the light faded from the sky and a small lantern mounted on the wall came

113

into its own. On the table between them, Giles's recorder revolved steadily, clicking each time it came to the end of a cassette, when a new one was rapidly inserted. And Caroline's pen sped over pages and pages of her notebook as the great man answered her eager questions, expounded his ideas, spoke of his plans. It was, had any of them known it, the most intimate and detailed interview Henri Duval was to give in his life.

More drinks were brought, a dish of *crudités*, a bowl of olives, and outside in the village behind them the church clock regularly chimed the quarter hours.

Caroline was enthralled, throwing in as many of her own questions as those Giles had prepared. As the time passed, a more personal note began to creep into question and reply, and she realised to her amusement that the great man, forgetting his exalted position and remembering only that he was a Frenchman and she an attractive girl, was beginning delicately to flirt with her. She had no way of knowing whether Giles realised this, though he had straightened very slightly in his chair, because Duval was cloaking his compliments by concealing them, without change of tone, in increasingly rapid French.

'It would give me great pleasure if you would have dinner with me,' he said softly, his eyes on the glass in his hand.

Caroline flashed a look at Giles, was unable

114

to see any reaction at all, and answered, 'I regret it would not be possible.'

'But we have more to discuss than the confines of this interview allows—and our conversation, in French as it would be, could not interest Monsieur your employer. Surely, once he had the information he has come for, he would excuse you?'

'I don't think—'

'I have never before discussed my work in detail with a foreigner and I find it fascinating. I should also like to enquire about some of your own great directors. I beg you, *mademoiselle*, allow me to insist.'

Caroline hesitated and said in English. He wants me to have dinner with him.'

'No way.'

Some demon in her prompted her to argue the point. 'You wouldn't mind, surely? He wants to discuss English films—'

'Tell it to the Marines,' said Giles succinctly.

'Marines?' repeated Duval, with a puzzled frown, and Caroline gave a little choke of laughter.

'I regret Monsieur does not care for the idea.'

'Is he your lover?' the Frenchman asked abruptly.

Her startled eyes flew from him to Giles and back again. 'Certainly not!'

'But would, perhaps, like to be?'

'*Monsieur*, I must protest!'

'Forgive me, *mademoiselle*, but if not he has no claim on you. After your hours of work, you are surely free.'

'You are not,' Giles said adamantly, 'going to have dinner with him, and that's an end to it.'

The interview was virtually over. Henri Duval appeared to have lost interest in everything but persuading Caroline to stay behind when Giles left. Tactfully, delicately, thankful for her idiomatic French, she managed to convey the impression that she would have been only too delighted to remain indefinitely, but Monsieur must understand that he who pays the piper calls the tune. Henri Duval's sad, spaniel eyes indicated that indeed he understood and at last, with a cursory handshake for Giles and a deep bow as he held Caroline's hand to his lips, he allowed them to take their leave.

There was a bubble of laughter inside her as she glanced at Giles's set face. 'Spoilsport!' she said—and only then did she realise how angry he was.

'No doubt I'm getting in your way now, but you've taken little enough notice of me all evening. May I remind you you were here in the role of interpreter, not to conduct the interview single-handed.'

'But you told me what you wanted to know. I—'

'You never so much as referred back to me,

116

did you? My presence seemed completely superfluous. Can you imagine what a fool I felt, sitting in silence while the two of you made sheep's eyes at each other?'

'Giles!' She stopped and stared at him.

'All that simpering and fluttering of eyelashes! No wonder he thought he was in with a chance! I'd never seen you in action before—it was masterly. I'm only sorry I had to put the damper on your little game.'

She said furiously, 'If I didn't know you better, I'd say you were jealous!'

He ignored her. 'You surely didn't expect me to believe you'd sit solemnly discussing the cinema all night? What do you take me for? "Am I your lover, or would I like to be?" Bloody nerve! That in itself—'

'You understood!' She stared at him whitely.

'Of course I understood. I never said I didn't, merely that I refuse to make a fool of myself speaking French.'

'You deliberately let me think—'

'My dear girl, spying, as you seem to consider it, never entered my head. I was hardly to know you'd set out to seduce the man!'

Blindly she swung at him, but he caught her wrist. 'On reflection, though, I should have guessed, because it's only strangers who turn you on, isn't it? Unknown men in the dark, people you've barely met?'

'Let go of me! Take your hand off me!' She

117

struggled ineffectually, but his grip didn't slacken.

'Be reasonable, now. I'm responsible to Adeline for your well-being and however much you fancied him, I could hardly let you waltz off into the blue with a dubious French—'

'*Dubious?*' she echoed furiously. 'Henri Duval?'

'Point taken—that was the wrong word. His intentions were never in the slightest doubt.'

'At least he had perfect manners, which is more than can be said of you!'

They stood facing each other, implacably hostile. Giles drew a long, steadying breath and said evenly, 'Now, if you're over your tantrum, we'll go and have some dinner.'

Holding tightly to her arm, he led her into the hotel and through to the restaurant. Caroline hadn't the strength to resist him. She would have liked to go straight to her room, but she realised she was empty and would not sleep until she had eaten.

Giles ordered the meal without consulting her—*pistou*, a thick vegetable soup, escalopes of veal stuffed with ham, salad, cheese and fruit. She ate because she had to, but she didn't touch the wine he poured for her. He made no comment, simply refilling his own glass when it was empty.

When she had finished the food on her plate, she pushed back her chair and without a word left the room. He caught up with her before the lift arrived.

'You're determined to go on behaving like a spoilt child?'

'How do you consider you're behaving?'

'With the utmost patience under trying circumstances.'

The lift stopped at their floor. On either side the corridor stretched, dimly lit at infrequent intervals. Caroline had the key ready in her hand and as she reached her door, inserted it swiftly and turned the lock.

'Just a moment.' Giles caught her arm and swung her round. 'Since you so obviously resent my spoiling your chances with Duval, perhaps I should offer myself as substitute. That would at least keep it in the family.'

She stared at him, struggling for breath. 'Of all the vile—'

Before she realised his intention he had reached behind her, turned the handle and pushed her into the room, closing the door behind them with a final-sounding click.

'Get out this minute!' she snapped.

'Outraged modesty? But we know better, don't we? You're not the unawakened little innocent Simon supposes, are you?'

He pulled her savagely against him, one hand moving up under her hair to hold her head rigid as his mouth came forcefully down on hers. And despite all the jumbled hatred, resentment and fury inside her, her treacherous body betrayed her. Of their own

119

accord her lips parted to admit the demand of his as he pressed her convulsively still closer and she helplessly responded to his insistent urgency.

For long, draining moments they clung together until shortness of breath forced her to turn her head aside and his hand slid inside her bodice, popping open the little buttons as it closed greedily round her breast. His lips were pulling gently at the lobe of her ear, and the frighteningly compulsive rhythms which her body had so spontaneously adopted in time with his were sucking her deeper and deeper into an eddying whirlpool of desire. Caught up in his increasing passion, she did not realise she was being gently, inexorably pushed backwards until she felt the hard edge of the bed behind her knees. And instantly panic came to her rescue. With a surge of strength she pushed him away.

'No!' she whispered. 'Giles, no! Please!'

He straightened, his hand still on her breast.

'What do you mean, no?'

'I—please go now.'

'*Go?*' He laughed harshly. 'You must be out of your mind! What's the matter?'

'Do you still think you'd have done better with the Frenchman? If so, I can—'

'Giles, please don't—' She pushed at his hand and it fell away.

'Isn't this maidenly modesty a little late? You haven't exactly been fighting me off,

120

have you?'

It was appallingly true. She could only shake her head helplessly.

'What the hell are you playing at, Caroline? You know damn well I want you, and all the signs were that it was mutual. Now, suddenly, it's "Don't touch me—I'm not that sort of girl!" Like hell you're not!'

'I can understand your being angry,' she said just above a whisper. 'I didn't mean to—to let you think I'd—'

'Go to bed with me?' he finished brutally. 'Then what the devil were you up to? Playing hot and cold is a dangerous game, you know. You deserve all you get.'

Impossible to explain that she was helpless to defend herself against his caresses. She didn't reply. He put a hand, none too gently, under her chin, forcing her head up until her eyes unwillingly met his.

'Well? You at least owe me an explanation for all this embarrassment. Why did you play me along like that? Do you really hate me so much that you'd—'

'No!' she broke in. 'At least, that wasn't why. It was just—'

'Just what?'

'I couldn't help it,' she whispered.

She felt his sudden stillness and when she forced herself to meet his eyes again it was to find them intent on her face with an entirely unreadable expression in them. At last his

121

hand dropped from her chin.

'Goodnight,' he said abruptly, and left her.

Caroline stood for several moments staring at the closed door. Then her eyes fell to the open front of her dress and her breast still mottled from his fondling. At the memory a shaft of desire, as sharp as it was unwelcome, lanced through her and she gave a little moan, slipping to the floor and burying her face in the soft white candlewick of the bedspread. But despite the turbulence inside her, she forced herself to go over everything that had passed between them, the erotic throbbing pressure of his body, the sensuous caress of his hands, the brutal dominance of his mouth. And she knew, starkly, that more than anything in the world she had wanted him to make love to her.

Yet even as the admission formed in her mind, she realised that hadn't been the way he'd phrased it. 'I want you', he'd said. And 'to go to bed with me'. Not a word about love. Of course not. It probably wasn't in Giles Guthrie's vocabulary.

As regards herself, he didn't even like her— nor she him, she reminded herself with burning shame. What had happened between them had been purely physical, and it was she who was to blame for having let it go so far.

Like a sleepwalker she started to undress, schooling herself to ignore the still insistent pulses of her awakened body, the throbbing in

122

her breast. It was as well she'd settled everything in her mind tonight, because she'd need strength to face him with composure the next morning. And there was the long drive back to St Luc ahead of them.

She climbed into bed, switched off the light, and lay for a long time staring blindly upwards in the dark. It was a physical effort to force her eyelids shut, but when she achieved it, she managed to sleep.

She awoke the next morning to excited French voices raised in dispute three floors below her, and as consciousness returned so did the flood of humiliation as she remembered her abject clinging to Giles. No wonder he despised her! She dragged herself out of bed, washed, dressed, put her few belongings back in the case.

When she reached the restaurant he was already at the table. He rose as she joined him, but she dared not meet his eyes.

'Did you sleep well?' he asked formally.

'Moderately.'

He made no comment and the waiter came with fresh rolls, coffee, chocolate. Giles passed her the sugar and from the corner of her eye she saw that his hand shook slightly. She felt it unwise to ask how he had slept.

For a few minutes they sat in silence, passing each other rolls and jam with almost exaggerated politeness. Perhaps, she thought numbly, he was just going to pretend nothing

123

had happened—and perhaps that was the best way.

But as the thought formed, he said suddenly, 'Caroline, there's something I have to say.' Instinctively she stiffened and he went on quickly, 'You probably don't want to talk about last night any more than I do, but bear with me just for a moment. If I'm to retain any self-respect at all, I have to apologise. I behaved appallingly. After talking pedantically about my responsibility towards you, I—'

He broke off and she saw his hand clench. 'You're not going to help me out, are you?' he commented wryly, as she didn't speak.

'I'm sorry too, Giles,' she said in a low voice. 'Obviously I gave you the impression—'

'Yes, well, that was my mistake. We always seem to end up on opposite sides of the fence, don't we? I was hoping we could have got through this expedition without any traumas, but it doesn't seem possible. Of course I over-reacted about Duval. There was no earthly reason why you shouldn't have had dinner with him. As it turned out you'd have probably been safer with him than you were with me.' The bitterness was back in his voice. 'And of course the interview was fabulous. You handled it brilliantly. My outburst was solely due to hurt pride.'

Still Caroline kept her eyes down. Despite the level-headedness of her conclusions the night before, his closeness was making it hard to control her breathing and the fluctuating colour came and went in her face.

'Can't you bring yourself even to look at me?'

Since she had no option she slowly raised her eyes to his, and for a moment their gaze held. She saw that his face was taut and his eyes shadowed, as though he hadn't slept. He accepted her scrutiny in silence and then smiled crookedly.

'There, that wasn't too bad, was it?'

Tentatively she smiled back and a flicker crossed his face. But all he said, briskly, was, 'If you've finished we might as well go.'

The awkwardness was still between them in the car, and Giles switched on the radio to bridge the long gaps in their conversation. At one point Caroline asked, 'How many copies will you want of the transcript?'

'I'd better have two. I'm afraid it will be a lot of work for you; you seemed almost to fill your notebook. You can take the cassettes, if they'd be any help.'

'Keep them for checking,' she said briefly, and the oblique reference to the fact that he did after all understand the language inevitably led both their minds back to their altercation.

'Is he your lover, or would he like to be?' Caroline's fingers tightened round her bag. She knew the answer now, beyond any doubt. And if, against all the odds, she had allowed

125

him to stay last night, his desire would have been slaked and he would have been free to let her go and move on elsewhere. Instead, the knowledge of her unattainability would probably stay with him, like the pearl within an oyster, a source of needling irritation.

Which, she thought flatly, was just too bad. At least he knew how to come to terms with his craving, and if need be no doubt he could assuage it elsewhere. For her, the needs and desires he had aroused had no way of being satisfied.

Adeline came out on to the terrace to meet them. 'Well, how did it go?' Her sharp eyes went from one of them to the other and Caroline wondered uneasily just how much they saw.

'Excellently,' Giles replied. 'Caroline was marvellous. She got him talking absolutely freely. We should have a veritable treasure-trove.'

'Fine.' Adeline glanced at the girl, but she made no comment. 'You'll stay for lunch, Giles?'

'Thank you, but no. I think I'll go straight to the boat.'

'Velma was asking when you'd be back. Perhaps she—'

'Make my excuses, would you, Adeline? I'd like to be alone for a while. Thanks again, Caroline.' And he was gone.

Adeline said softly, 'Well, well! And what

about you, child, if you haven't lost your tongue? Did your idol come up to expectations?'

'He was very pleasant. We certainly got masses of information.'

'Which presumably will now have to be typed out. It'll take some time, I don't doubt.'

'There's the rest of today and tomorrow, unless you need me.'

'But you'll want to relax, surely? The last few days must have been tiring.'

'I'd rather do it straight away, while it's fresh in my mind. Then I'll be clear by Monday.'

Adeline shrugged. 'Just as you like, of course.'

So Caroline set to work at once, holding her memory suspended as she meticulously translated all the thoughts and ideas which had come pouring from the famous director, and ignoring the odd scribbles where she had started to take down one of the encroaching compliments before she realised what it was. And by late Sunday evening three neat piles of typescript lay on her desk. Now she had only to deliver two of them to Giles. It would be a long time before she would be able to re-read the one she was keeping for herself.

CHAPTER SEVEN

Caroline had hoped that Giles would come over as he so often did and she could hand him the typescripts with the minimum of fuss. But he did not appear on the Monday, and when Tuesday afternoon arrived with still no sign of him, she reluctantly decided she would have to deliver them herself.

She had often passed the gate to Le Sirocco on her way to the bus-stop, but the villa itself wasn't visible from the road and when she had walked down the gravelled drive between the pine trees, she found it was considerably smaller than Mimosa, a low, single-storey house in typical Provençal style with Moorish archways and terracotta shutters against the deep cream stonework.

'Monsieur is by the pool,' said the dumpy little woman who answered the door. 'If Mademoiselle would come this way—'

She led Caroline across the hall and into a large salon which ran across the back of the house. Its far wall was composed of sliding windows and immediately outside, beyond a wide, paved terrace, was a small pool. A couple of sun-loungers were set up to the side and on one of these Giles was lying with closed eyes.

Caroline said, only half truthfully, 'He is

expecting me.'

The woman nodded and withdrew and she walked slowly through the open windows and stood looking down at him. His hair was damp from a recent swim and a few drops of water still glistened on the smooth brown skin. Her eyes went slowly over him, the powerful column of his throat, the broad shoulders, flat stomach and strong brown legs. And, deliberately interrupting her examination, she said hesitantly, 'Giles?'

His eyes opened at once, but for a moment he didn't move. Then he stood up. 'Hello, Caroline.'

'I've brought the transcript.'

'Already? I thought it would take you days. Sit down.' He pulled forward the vacant sun-lounger. Without seeming to run away, she could only do as he suggested. She handed him the papers and lay back, closing her eyes.

For some minutes there was silence, broken only by the rustling pages as he flicked his way through them. 'This is marvellous,' he said then. 'A verbatim report.' He paused and added, 'I didn't understand quite everything, you know. Certain phrases left me groping and he'd moved on before I had time to wrestle with them. This sets it out so clearly I can even see where I was floundering.' He laid the papers in the shade under his chair. 'Can I get you a drink?'

'Orange or lemon would be lovely.'

129

He went through into the salon and Caroline heard the clink of ice. There must be a refrigerated bar in there. The glass he handed her was beaded with condensation, almost too cold to hold. She sipped the drink and put it on the ground beside her.

'How's Simon?' asked Giles.

'Fine, thank you.'

'Didn't miss you too much while you were away?'

'I shouldn't think so.'

'We must have that day on the boat I promised you both. Time's moving along. I suppose you'll be leaving at the end of the month?'

'We should have been, but there's some big party at the beginning of July, so we're staying on an extra week for that.'

'Ah yes, Jeremy Tait's. Adeline wouldn't want to miss that.'

Caroline thought of the London flat awaiting her return. How bleak and lonely it would seem, after all these weeks in the centre of a family. Giles no doubt would stay on for the rest of the summer working on his French series.

He reached for his glass and she heard the ice tinkle. His next words took her completely by surprise. 'You like fish, don't you? Have you ever tried *bouillabaisse*?'

She struggled to regroup her thoughts. 'I don't think so.'

'It's one of the local dishes, of course, probably the most famous. There's an excellent restaurant up the coast where they make a speciality of it. I wondered if perhaps you'd care to sample it?'

Her heart started thudding in slow, suffocating beats. 'Giles, I really don't think—'

'Look, I simply want to make some small gesture of appreciation for all this.' His hand sketched a movement in the direction of the pile of papers. 'Of course there'll be a cheque, but that's rather impersonal.'

She said carefully, 'Don't you think it's better if we keep things on that level?'

'The fact is I still have a conscience about what happened. I was hoping this could be "I'm sorry" as well as "thank you". Please, Caroline. Call a truce and let me absolve myself.'

She hesitated, aware of conflict inside her where there shouldn't be any. It ought to have been perfectly simple to hold to her refusal; she was under no obligation to help him soothe his ruffled conscience. Yet she knew, ruefully, that she wanted to have dinner with him. And surely this time they would both be on their guard and there would be no chance of a repetition of the scene at Ste Emmanuelle.

'Please,' said Giles again at her continuing silence.

She reached a decision. 'All right. Thank

131

you,' she added as an afterthought.

'Thank *you*.'

It was arranged he should book a table for the next evening and collect her at seven-thirty. Caroline was very thoughtful as she walked home.

Reactions at the villa were mixed when she announced that she would not be in for dinner the following evening.

'*Giles* is taking you out?' Velma repeated sharply. 'Why on earth?'

'To thank me for the work I did for him.'

'He's paying you, isn't he?' She managed to make it sound an insult.

Simon said mildly, 'It won't be much of a treat, surely, considering the way you feel about him.'

Adeline Stevens said nothing at all, but Caroline was acutely aware of her assessing gaze.

The following evening she selected a backless white chiffon dress with softly draped bodice, her only jewellery the plain gold chain. Unwilling to greet Giles under the curious gaze of the family, she went out to wait for him on the terrace. How long ago it seemed, that first evening when she had rounded the corner to meet him face to face. Impossible to have imagined, then, that she would ever contemplate dining alone with him. So absorbed was she in her thoughts that she didn't hear him approach until he said softly,

'You look very lovely.'

To her confusion she felt her colour rise. Compliments between them were something new. 'Thank you,' she murmured, and as he slipped a hand under her arm, went with him along the drive to the gate where the blue Peugeot was waiting. Giles opened the door for her and walked round to his own side. He was wearing a cream jacket with caramel-coloured shirt and trousers, and the light colours emphasised the blackness of his hair and the deep tan of his skin.

'I bookcd the table for nine, so we've plenty of time for drinks first. I hope you're hungry— the servings are on the generous side.'

Caroline settled back in her seat, aware of his efforts to put her at ease and gradually feeling the defensiveness he always aroused begin to fade. It was a glorious summer evening and she resolved to relax, forget just for tonight the part Giles had unwittingly played in her life, and allow herself to enjoy his company.

It was easier than she would have believed possible. They drove first to a little bar-restaurant which was built at the end of a long jetty right out over the sea. The foundations rocked slightly under them against the slap of the waves and coloured lights were strung above the tables and reflected in the darkening water below. Caroline was aware of the envious glances she attracted from women at the other tables and felt a flicker of pride in her escort, and satisfaction that his own glance never seemed to stray.

If only he wasn't who he was! she caught herself thinking wistfully, before clamping down on the thought and reminding herself that this evening was simply the repayment of a debt, a unique occasion which would never be repeated.

But it was no wonder, she reflected, that women found Giles attractive. When he set out to please, as he obviously had this evening, there was a charm of manner, an air of polished *savoir-faire* which could well prove irresistible. Except, of course, to herself. Even so, she found herself responding to it, seeing his delighted surprise at her occasional witticism and the seemingly genuine admiration in his eyes.

When they had finished their drinks they drove on again, up into the mountains this time, where the sweeping headlights provided the only illumination in the dark wildness and the trees leaned closely over the road. The restaurant was at the end of a long, uneven track, built on the edge of a cliff which jutted out from the coast. There was a small dance floor beyond the canopy of the restaurant itself, with only the stars overhead.

The tables were covered with red and white checked cloths and a vine grew over the low ceiling. At the open side of the restaurant near

134

the dance floor a string quartet played unobtrusively.

'There are very few restaurants which have dancing,' Giles commented. 'To the French eating is a serious business, but this place is geared to the tourist trade, so they've made a concession.'

Caroline's eyes swung back from her delighted inspection to find him watching her. 'Glad you decided to come?' he asked with a smile.

'Very glad!'

'Wait till you see the *bouillabaisse*!'

It was certainly a magnificent spectacle. A tureen of soup was set on the table, together with a basket of crisply toasted slices of bread spread with garlic. Then came the fish—pink fish, white fish, still with heads attached and a baleful eye—tiny crabs, chunks of eel, curly prawns. To Caroline's relief the waiter filleted them at Giles's request. Then, following his instructions, she placed a handful of bread in the bottom of her bowl before he ladled the soup over it. Only when that was finished were the fish eaten, accompanied by potatoes boiled in the stock and creamy mayonnaise.

'Well done!' said Giles with a laugh when she finally laid down her knife and fork. 'A very creditable effort!'

'It was delicious. I thoroughly enjoyed it.'

Fresh strawberries followed, their cool sweetness soothing away the savoury taste of the highly seasoned soup. Giles ordered coffee and liqueurs.

'Would you like to dance?'

She hesitated, glancing outside to where a few couples, indistinct in the dimness, drifted slowly to the dreamy music.

Without waiting for an answer, Giles stood up and held her chair for her as she came uncertainly to her feet.

'I'm really too full to move!' she murmured protestingly.

'You needn't move very much,' he answered, and the remembered tingle ran over her skin. An evening apart, she reminded herself hastily. Just one dance couldn't do any harm.

But as his arms came round her she started to tremble and he gently drew her closer, holding her firmly but lightly as they began to circle the floor.

It seemed imperative to break the spell, shatter their increasing intimacy with ordinary, everyday words that held no hint of romance. Caroline asked jerkily, 'Whereabouts in London do you live?' and felt his surprise.

'In Kensington. Why?'

'I just wondered. In a flat?'

'Yes.'

'Alone? I mean—' she felt herself grow hot—'have you anyone to clean and cook for you?'

'I have. Next question?'

She bit her lip but plunged on. 'What about your family?'

'They live in Dorset—mother, father, married sister. And before you ask, I was educated at Winchester and King's College, Cambridge. Anything else?'

'Do you—'

'Caroline,' he interrupted softly.

'Yes?'

'Be quiet, there's a good girl.' And he pulled her still closer. The only sounds were the low humming strings of the instruments, an occasional scrape of a shoe from the other dancers, the ceaseless slapping of the sea far below them.

'You know,' he murmured into her hair, 'I'm enjoying our truce. Shall we seal it in the approved manner? It surely ought to be possible for us to kiss each other without losing our tempers. Let's try.'

'No!' she said breathlessly.

'I rather think—yes.' He gently turned her averted face towards him. His mouth was tender, questioning rather than demanding, but deep and strong, a world away from Simon's butterfly kisses. Her arms ached to go round him, but instead she stood unmoving, rigid as a statue.

After several long minutes he released her. 'That,' he said unevenly, 'was just to say thank you.'

Still she didn't move. 'But this isn't!' And as

137

he reached for her again she went to him as though released by a spring, arms flying round his neck, hands feverishly caressing the back of his neck, his ears, his hair. His hands slid down her bare back, straining her against the thrust of his body, fondling, compelling as the deep primeval rhythm took hold of them. The force of his mouth was hurting her lips, but she gave herself up to it gladly, exulting in the iron hardness of his thighs, the sensuous caress of his hands. And she closed her mind to the small voice whose warning every nerve in her body longed to ignore, blotted it out till it rose inside her clarioning its alarm bells and forcing itself to her attention. With a little groan she pushed him from her and turned away, leaning on the parapet with her face in her hands.

Giles was close behind her, his hands on her shoulders. 'What is it, Caroline? Nothing can possibly be wrong this time?'

The oyster and the pearl, she thought numbly. He hadn't after all been prepared to let her go without one more try. When force hadn't succeeded, he'd tried the soft approach and she'd fallen for it. How neatly she'd played into his hands!

She said shakily, 'You're very determined, aren't you?'

'You could put it that way.' After a moment he added, 'We have a truce, remember.'

'Part of it was to keep your distance.'

'Do you really want me to?'

138

'Yes!' she said fiercely. 'Yes, yes, yes!'

'It's pointless to deny we enjoy kissing each other, so why do we always have this backlash afterwards? Does Simon have to put up with this dramatic withdrawal?'

She didn't answer and after a moment he went on, 'It's almost as though you enjoy it in spite of yourself; as if part of you is determined to hold me at bay while another part wants me as much as I want you.'

'Want—is that all you think about, *wanting*?'

'Almost all, when I'm with you.' He turned her to face him, gently pulling her hands from her face. 'Don't fight me, Caroline. I hoped we'd finished with that.'

'You thought the change of tactics would work?'

'Tactics?' he repeated blankly. 'Look, I simply don't understand. One moment you're all I could hope for, and the next the barriers are up again and there's no way I can get through to you. Why? There has to be some reason for it.'

Over in the far corner of the dance floor someone laughed softly.

'Caroline.' Giles shook her gently. 'I have to know. *Is* there something concrete behind all this?'

'Yes.' The word was simply an outgoing breath.

'Then for God's sake tell me what it is, so I can put it right.'

139

She shook her head. 'You can't, Giles. It can never be put right.' And at the realisation a terrible bleakness washed over her and she almost cried out.

'I can't accept that,' he said after a moment.

Desperation added an edge to her voice. 'I'm afraid you'll have to.'

'Then at least tell me what it is.'

'There's no point.'

'And that's all you have to say?'

She nodded, fighting back the tears that were threatening to deluge her.

He said wearily, 'Very well,' and led her back to the table. With dulled eyes she stared at the cups of coffee they had abandoned fifteen minutes earlier. She'd been happy then, but it had been a false happiness. She should never have relaxed her guard, not allowed herself to forget for one moment who her partner was.

'So much for the truce,' Giles said expressionlessly, pouring hot coffee into both their cups.

She put a hand to her mouth to hide its trembling. 'This evening was a mistake. I should never have agreed to come.'

'But it seemed to be going so well. You were enjoying it, surely?'

'Yes, but I—thought you understood—'

'That my advances would be unwelcome?' His voice was hard. 'I managed to persuade myself otherwise—probably because I have difficulty keeping my hands off you, as no doubt you've noticed.'

'And you're used to getting your own way.'

'I suppose I am, yes.'

Shakily Caroline exhaled her held breath. So he admitted it. His pride hadn't let him accept that she would continue to hold out against him.

'You still won't tell me the origin of all this?'

She shook her head. Though he was probably entitled to an explanation, any mention of her father at this point would cause her to break down completely.

His hand clenched on the table. 'Then why the hell do you respond at all? To make me think that perhaps this time—' He broke off and slowly straightened in his chair. 'Sorry. Subject closed. More coffee?'

'I think I'd like to go home.'

'That makes two of us.'

Thank heaven for the car radio, though rousing martial music would have suited her better than the plaintive love songs which came over the air. Why had she submitted to this evening? Would she never learn that however clearly her mind assessed Giles Guthrie, her body unashamedly wanted him?

Wanted—his word. Yet what other was there? She could hardly use 'love'. A little choked sound escaped her and she turned it, not too successfully, into a cough. Giles's hands tightened on the steering wheel, but he

141

made no comment, and in continuing silence they dropped down into Avenue Pascal and drew up at the gate of the Villa Mimosa.

Caroline said rapidly, 'Thank you for the *bouillabaisse*. It was an experience I shall never forget.'

'I'm sure it was.'

She fumbled the car door open. Giles made no attempt to help her, nor to accompany her down the path. He probably assumed that she wouldn't welcome either his help or his company.

In the privacy of her bedroom, face muffled in her pillow, she sobbed brokenheartedly for a very long time.

CHAPTER EIGHT

The days crawled past. Caroline's recently revived appetite had wilted and the shadows were back under her eyes. She made a valiant attempt to conceal her unhappiness—indeed, to deny its existence—but that it was apparent was noticeable in Simon's renewed attentions, and she found his gentle care of her soothing and unexpectedly precious.

During this time she threw herself almost frantically into work on Adeline's book, using a lot of her free time to correct the manuscript and look up obscure references. And though she daily dreaded and yet looked for Giles's appearance at the villa, he did not come.

One morning she reached the study to find her employer already at her desk, the phone to her ear. As Caroline hesitated, Adeline beckoned her inside and at the same moment said into the mouthpiece: 'Giles? Where have you been hiding yourself?'

Caroline felt the colour rush into her cheeks. She turned her back and went through the motions of sorting some pages, the paper rustling in her suddenly shaking hands.

'Be that as it may,' Adeline went on, in response to his reply, 'I don't usually have to go to the length of issuing formal invitations to you, but on this occasion it appears necessary. Your presence is requested at dinner on Friday.'

Though Caroline wasn't looking at her, it was clear by her voice that she was smiling. 'So you hadn't forgotten? Good. Well, it wouldn't seem like a birthday if you weren't there, so I had to make sure. No, only family as usual, unless anyone arrives unexpectedly. Fine. Come as early as you can.'

The receiver clicked into place and Adeline said, 'You heard, I presume?'

'It's your birthday?'

'On Friday, yes.' She paused. 'Is anything wrong, child? Between you and Giles? You haven't seemed yourself this last week, and it's not like him to keep away so long. It all dates

143

from the evening you spent together.'

'There was a—slight misunderstanding,' Caroline answered with difficulty.

'Don't be deceived by all that smoothness. Underneath it, he's as vulnerable as the next man.'

Caroline's voice shook. 'Surely it's Velma you should be telling.'

'Hm. Very well, if you don't want to talk about it, we won't pursue the matter. Were you able to check that point we came unstuck on yesterday?' And the conversation veered to safer topics.

However, the subject came up again with Simon. 'You know Giles will be here on Friday?' he asked quietly as they sat alone on the terrace. She nodded and he reached for her hand.

'He upset you last week, didn't he? I thought at the time it was unwise of you to go out with him.' He raised her hand and brushed his lips across her fingers. 'Don't worry, poppet, I'll see he keeps his distance.'

He was as good as his word, and when Friday came, waited for her on the landing so that she should have moral support in her meeting with Giles. As they went into the salon together Giles turned from the window. Caroline felt a stabbing pain go through her and her fingers unconsciously tightened on Simon's arm. But all he said, gravely, was 'Good evening, Caroline, Simon,' and turned to greet Humphrey Betts, who had flown back for the birthday celebration.

Dinner took the form of a barbecue on the terrace, and though the Perriers laid out all the food on wrought iron tables, they then withdrew, leaving them to cook for themselves. Humphrey, Giles and Simon officiated, though Simon kept returning to Caroline's side like a mother hen checking on its chick. There was steak, blackened on the outside, red within, with the smoky charcoal flavour that was unlike any other. And garlic sausage, small tender chops, mushrooms and great bowls of ready-mixed salad. The crickets were humming and the night-scented flowers mingled their perfume with the cooking smells, while great fragile moths blundered round the lamps and festooned the panes of the window.

Above the glow of the embers, Giles's face was set as he turned the meat. It seemed to Caroline that he was quieter than usual. Perhaps he was as embarrassed in her company as she was in his. From time to time she felt his eyes on her, but every time she glanced up he looked away.

When the meal was over they settled down with coffee, Simon close by Caroline's side. She felt an upsurge of affection for him. They were almost back on the London footing, she realised, and wasn't sure how to interpret the fact.

'You're becoming quite a recluse, Giles!'

145

Velma was complaining. 'You haven't been to nearly as many of the parties as usual.'

He smiled slightly. 'I'm sorry. I find I'm outgrowing them.'

'Nor have you taken me out on the boat for weeks—and don't tell me you're outgrowing that!'

'Ah.' Giles looked across at Simon. 'You asked some time ago about coming out for a day. As Velma says, I've been letting things slip rather. Put it down to absorption in this series I'm working on. However, if you'd like to come, perhaps we can fix a day.'

'How about it, Caro?' Simon asked gently. 'Would you like a day on the boat?'

They were all looking at her and she could only murmur a confused assent.

'Sunday?' Giles suggested. 'We could go up round the coast and perhaps have lunch on one of the islands.'

When they had finished their coffee, Simon excused himself and Caroline. As they walked down into the garden, he said anxiously, 'You do want to go on the boat, don't you? She's an absolute beauty and capable of going at a fair lick.'

'Yes, of course. It'll be—very interesting.' At least Velma could be relied on to keep Giles occupied, and she would have Simon beside her.

'Sunday's ideal,' he was going on, 'because Velma and I have to lunch with some friends of the parents tomorrow. It'll be a bit of a drag, but at least we'll have the next day to look forward to.'

He pulled her gently against him and she stood quietly in the circle of his arms, feeling his cheek against her hair. The certainty that no response was expected of her was strangely comforting after the tempestuousness of Giles's embrace. She jerked involuntarily at the memory and Simon's mouth moved gently over her closed lips. 'Sweet, sweet Caroline,' he said softly.

By the time they returned to the terrace, Giles had gone.

The following day, left to her own devices, Caroline spent the morning by the pool, but some friends of Adeline's were also there, and although they were friendly enough she felt awkward in their presence. After lunch, therefore, she decided to go to the beach instead.

The little bay was as quiet and secluded as ever, though round the corner towards St Luc more and more people were thronging the narrow strip of sand as the holiday crowds steadily increased. There was little more than a week left now before their return to London, and despite the loneliness awaiting her there, she was glad. In London she would only be with Adeline during the day, when Giles was unlikely to visit her.

Above her, his voice said quietly, 'Hello,

147

Caroline.'

Too late she remembered that his villa also had access to this beach.

'Very quiet for the time of year,' he added facetiously, dropping his towel on the sand.

'Giles, I—'

'—wish I'd get the hell out of it. Yes, I know. I'm sorry to force myself on you, but it's partly your own fault. I thought I could accept your ultimatum of no explanations, but I found last night I couldn't.' He settled himself beside her and she turned her head away, staring along the flat silver sand to the cliffs that enclosed the bay.

'I know you put it down to injured pride,' he went on evenly as she didn't speak, 'but nevertheless since you obviously bear me some personal grudge, I must insist on knowing what it is.'

He's right, she thought dully. I at least owe him that. Across the burning blue of the sky a gull drifted like a feather in some current of air. Her voice seemed to come from equally far away.

'McDermott Cain was my father.'

There was total silence. Then he said very quietly, 'Oh God. And of course you blame me for his death.'

She sat unmoving, head still averted, and the seconds ticked past.

'I did write,' he said finally. 'Did you get my letter?'

148

'Something came from the B.B.C. I threw it away.'

'The wreath as well?'

Her voice rocked. 'I don't know what happened to that. Still, it was mentioned in the press, I believe.'

'You think that's why I sent it?'

'Wasn't it?'

Giles said quietly, 'Your father was a fine man, Caroline. I admired him enormously.'

She spun round. 'How can you say that, when you deliberately set out to humiliate him?'

He shook his head decisively. 'Not humiliate, no. I couldn't have done if I'd tried. But I had to ask searching questions, that was my job. He knew that when he agreed to appear on the programme, and he wouldn't have thanked me for any kid-glove treatment.'

It was true, and the realisation discomfited her. It seemed that in this respect Giles had understood her father better than she had. She said in a low voice, 'You made him doubt himself, and his faith in other people. It was unforgivable.'

'Surely it was the boys who let him down who did that.'

'But you flung it in his face, and it was—it was the last—' She caught her lip fiercely between her teeth.

Giles said very gently, 'Did you know he was unwell before we went on the air?'

Her eyes widened. 'Then surely there was

149

even more reason—'

He raised his hand. 'I wanted to call a doctor, but he wouldn't hear of it. I told him the programme would be a strain and I didn't feel he was up to it, but he insisted he was all right and that I mustn't tone down the interview in any way. "It's only a touch of indigestion, damn it!" he said, and he was so convincing that I believed him.'

Caroline didn't—couldn't—speak.

'Ironically enough,' Giles went on slowly, 'I'd always wanted to meet him. I'd read all his books, cut his articles out of newspapers and so on. He always struck me as being so intrinsically *good*, which is probably an old-fashioned concept these days, but you know what I mean.'

She lay down suddenly, rolling on to her stomach and burying her head in her arms.

'Caroline—don't, please!' There was an odd, tender note in his voice that she had never heard before, and his hand on her shoulder was hesitant. 'Doesn't what I've told you make any difference?'

It did, of course, but after all the months of recriminations it was too soon to gauge how much. She wanted to throw herself into his anus, to sob away the hurt and hatred while he stroked her hair and told her everything would be all right. But the curtain of restraint between them couldn't easily be discarded and she hesitated too long. He withdrew his hand

150

and said bitterly, 'And I was so sure I could sort out what was wrong. All right, Caroline, you've proved your point. I shan't bother you again.'

She did raise her head then. 'Giles—' but her voice was drowned by Velma's from the path above the beach.

'So that's where you are! Simon, they're down here. Both of them.'

Caroline hid her head again. Her face was ravaged by tears and she couldn't let them see. Simon's voice said enquiringly, 'Caro?'

And then Giles's: 'I should leave her for a minute or two, Simon. She has a headache.'

'Poor love! The sun won't be helping.' He sat down next to her and it was his hand, not Giles's, that gently stroked her hair. 'I wish I could have stayed with you on your free day, but Mother insisted we went to the Varleys'.'

'Come on, now, baby brother!' Velma said lazily. 'It wasn't as much of a hardship as all that, with Amy making goo-goo eyes at you!'

'Amy Varley?' Giles interjected. 'She's only about fourteen, isn't she?'

'Seventeen, actually, and she follows Simon round like a little dog.'

'Don't be ridiculous, Velma.' Simon sounded uncomfortable.

'You know it's true; she always has done. She's a quiet, timid little thing, but her eyes speak for her.'

Giles gave a hard laugh. 'It's not like you to

151

be so perceptive, my love!'

'I'd never taken much notice of her before. Today I was bored out of my mind and hadn't anything better to do. It struck me that she has a great look of Caroline before her metamorphosis. Undo this buckle for me, will you, Giles? Grandmother's topless ban doesn't apply here, thank God. If it worries you, Simon, you'll just have to look the other way.'

Caroline lay motionless, wishing she could remember where her sunglasses were. Could she reach them and put them on before anyone saw her face? She stretched out a hand tentatively and found them at once. Carefully she sat up, slipping on the glasses and welcoming their dark disguise.

Giles, sitting slightly in front with Velma, turned and looked at her.

'Better?'

'Yes, thank you.'

His eyes searched her face briefly, then Velma murmured something and reached up to pull him down beside her. Caroline surprised in herself a shaft of unmistakable jealousy.

I'm in love with him! she thought, and the idea was so overwhelming that it stunned her. Cautiously she explored it further. On reflection it had probably been building up for some time. At least part of the antagonism she had felt must have been a form of self-defence. Now that he had explained about her father,

152

the last obstacle had been removed and she was free to recognise it.

'Doesn't it make a difference?' he had asked. Oh, why had Velma come just at that moment? Because of course it did—all the difference in the world! He had admired her father, been concerned about him that last evening. If her grief hadn't been so intense she would have realised that it was her own need to lash out, to blame someone for what had happened, that had been at the root of her hostility. It had been an instinctive rather than a rational reaction. If she had read the letter he had sent instead of hurling it unopened into the fire, her bitterness might have been dispelled straight away instead of festering on for so long. If, if—

But suppose that she had accepted before she came to France that Giles wasn't to blame. How would things have been between them then? She would have had no reason not to tell him straightaway who she was. And, she thought painfully, without the spur of her hostility to needle him, he would probably have taken no interest in her at all. What had intrigued him had been her relentless antagonism, for which he could find no reason. Pleasant, friendly girls were two a penny and his for the asking.

Nevertheless, for whatever reason, she *had* interested him, and their first, anonymous embrace had obviously shaken him. Probably the second occasion, at Ste Emmanuelle, had been partly to satisfy himself that it had been a fluke. In fact it had proved the exact opposite. Though they had been furious with each other, their mutual desire had been almost overwhelming. But, she reminded herself, sitting motionless on the sand, Giles had never mentioned love, nor had he given any indication of loving her. Wanting, yes; it was a word he had used more than once. But wanting wasn't loving, and the fact had never been so agonisingly apparent.

Behind their screen of dark glass her eyes moved longingly over him, the rippling muscles of back and shoulders under the smooth brown skin, the way his hair grew into the nape of his neck, the tilt of his head as he bent it to Velma's seductive murmurings.

Did he kiss Velma the way he kissed her? Yes, she thought chokingly, he probably did, or she wouldn't have the confidence to be as possessive towards him as she was.

Stiffly she turned her head to look at Simon, stretched out on his back beside her: fair hair bleached almost white by the sun, small inconsequential moustache and colourless lashes.

She stood up suddenly, startling the other three, and ran past them into the water, splashing it out of her way until the pressure against her legs was too strong and then dropping down into it, welcoming the shock of

154

its relative coldness on her sun-warmed skin. She began to swim strongly and steadily towards the far cliffs. Somehow, she thought, she would have to recreate that vital, interrupted moment of half an hour ago. She must let Giles know she accepted what he said, that there was no longer any barrier between them. Farther than that she dared not go, until she saw his reaction. But the move would have to come from her; he had told her unequivocally that he would not approach her again. And perhaps, now the mystery of her enmity was solved, she would hold no further interest for him.

She turned on to her back, saw that the others had followed her into the sea, and lay treading water watching them come after her, Velma dark and seal-like close behind Giles, Simon trailing slightly. Then when they had almost reached her, she turned turtle and struck out again for the shore. Laughing and protesting breathlessly, they too veered inland and minutes later the four of them lay gasping on the hot sand at the far end of the bay.

'Such energy!' Velma exclaimed when she could speak. 'What brought that on?'

'A touch of symbolism,' Caroline answered, aware of Giles's quick glance. 'Washing away the last of my—headache.' She looked across at him, he had turned away. Velma's bare breasts were rising and falling with her rapid breathing. Surrounded by golden-brown skin,

155

their whiteness was startling, emphasising their nakedness more than a uniform tan would have done. Was this display for Giles's benefit? And how was he reacting to it? Perhaps it was not the first time he had seen Velma like this. Had they—?

Caroline stumbled to her feet and began to run back along the sand to the place where they had left their things. She ignored their protesting voices and kept going until, reaching her towel, she flopped face down on it and lay panting with her exertion. She was not at all sure that she liked being in love.

'Whatever's got into you, Caro?' Simon grumbled breathlessly as he dropped down beside her. 'I've never known you so unpredictable!'

She opened one eye to look back along the beach and saw that Giles and Velma were coming more slowly, their arms round each other. Had she lost her chance with him, or hadn't she ever had one?

'It's boring to be predictable,' she said.

'I don't know about that. It leads to a much more comfortable existence.'

'You shouldn't want to be comfortable at your age!'

He rolled over on his stomach and peered into her face. 'A very profound statement! What's wrong with comfort?'

'It dulls your sense of adventure.'

He smiled. 'I'm not sure I have one anyway.'

156

'What haven't you got?' Velma asked behind them.

'A sense of adventure. Caro says it gets dulled with comfort.'

'Well, I've no intention of living in discomfort to prove it. What do you say, lover mine?'

'Comfortable or not, you're an adventuress all right!'

'You brute! That's not the same thing at all!' She lashed out at him playfully, but he held her off with one hand and she collapsed, laughing, on top of him, the length of her long bare legs over his.

Where could she run to this time? Caroline wondered numbly. But almost at once Giles tipped Velma off and she sat up and began to towel-dry her hair.

'A week today is Jeremy's party,' she remarked, 'and a couple of days after that Grandmother's going home. I don't know whether to stay or not. What are you doing, Simon?'

'I think I'll go back to London.'

'To be with Caroline, of course.'

'If she wants me, comfortable and unadventurous as I am!'

Caroline smiled and ruffled his hair.

'You're staying, aren't you, Giles?' Velma persisted. 'Would you like me to keep you company?'

'Actually I'm not sure how long I'll be here.'

'But your programme doesn't start till the autumn schedules at the end of September.'

'Even so, there's plenty of work to put in first.' He paused. 'Did either of you know Caroline's father was McDermott Cain?'

Caroline caught her breath.

Simon said, 'Really? Why didn't you tell us?'

And Velma, at the same time, 'Wasn't he the man who—?'

'Yes,' Giles answered quietly. 'He died virtually on my programme. So you see Caroline was quite justified in criticising my interviewing methods.'

'But it wasn't your fault!' Velma objected. 'I mean, it was a dreadful thing, but she can hardly blame you, surely?'

'All the same, I didn't make his last few minutes particularly—comfortable. That word again.'

Caroline said awkwardly, 'You couldn't have known—'

But Simon was exclaiming, 'This is incredible, Caro! I'd no idea! I mean, he was famous, wasn't he? You must be very proud of him.'

'Yes,' she answered flatly. 'Very proud and very fond. It—distorted things for a while.'

'And you couldn't bear to talk about him. I can understand that. No wonder you were so upset when we first met!'

'And when she came here, I was a constant

158

reminder.' Giles's voice was bitter.

'You didn't realise who she was?'

'No. He never referred to his daughter by name, and "Cain" isn't unusual enough to have made me wonder.'

'So how did you find out?'

Caroline said, 'I told him. But I do realise—'

'—It must have been quite a shaker,' Simon commented.

'It was.'

Velma started to brush her hair. 'I remember Grandmother saying you were very uptight at the time. You wanted to cancel the rest of the series, didn't you, but Brian wouldn't hear of it. And he was right, of course. For the next few weeks the whole nation was glued to the programme.'

'You suggest,' said Giles dangerously, 'that I should kill off a few more of my guests, to help the ratings?'

'Darling, of course not! I mean, you didn't—'

'Stop it!' Caroline said sharply.

'God, I'm sorry, Caroline. That was brutal.' Giles ran a hand over his face. 'I think this conversation has gone on long enough. I'm going back to the villa for a shower.'

He stood up, shook the sand from his towel and slung it over his shoulder. Then he looked down at Caroline, sitting frozen with Simon's arm comfortingly round her.

'Will you still be coming on the boat

tomorrow, or—?'

'I'll come.' She couldn't lose the chance of being near him, of perhaps having the opportunity to put things right.

'Then I promise not to do or say anything to upset you.'

Velma's puzzled eyes went from Giles's face to Caroline's, but something in his manner prevented her from either questioning his remark or following him as he turned and walked briskly to the steps.

'That all sounded very solemn.'

'So it should. There was no need to upset her now, either. I can't imagine why he brought the subject up at all.'

'But it's not like Giles to be so—Oh well.' She broke off with a shrug. 'He was upset himself when it all happened. I suppose it brought it back to him too.'

She stood up and slipped on her bikini top. 'Must make myself respectable before I reappear *chez Grandmère!* Are you coming up?'

'Yes, I think so.' Simon removed his arm from Caroline's shoulders, and helped her to her feet. 'You're shivering, sweetie. A hot shower will be the answer. Your headache hasn't come back, has it?'

'No, I'm all right.' But she was glad of his support as they went up the long, shallow flight of steps to the villa garden. Lydia and Humphrey Betts were just emerging from the trees round the pool, accompanied by the two couples with whom Caroline had passed the morning. They merged into one group and she was thankful that the general chat obviated the need for her to speak.

All at once she felt very tired. It had been a traumatic afternoon, the conversation with Giles followed so closely by the realisation of her love for him. And despite several attempts, she had not been able to let him know her change of attitude.

There was an envelope addressed to her on the hall table.

'Monsieur Guthrie brought it earlier,' Berthe Perrier told her. 'He was looking for you, *mademoiselle.* I said I thought you had gone to the beach. He found you?'

'Yes, thank you, *madame.* He found me.'

Her mouth was dry as she went into her room and tore open the envelope. Although it had been written before their fatal conversation, perhaps there might be something in it to give her hope. But the note, folded round a cheque, was formal to the point of stiffness.

'Dear Caroline: Herewith the cheque which I agreed with Adeline to cover your work on the Henri Duval interview. I'm most grateful for your help in this matter. Sincerely, Giles.'

She read it through again and then, with a sigh, laid it down on the dressing-table and went to run her bath.

CHAPTER NINE

There was a change in the weather the next morning. When Caroline opened the shutters after a restless night, it was to find that the blue had left the sky and down in the garden bushes were bending and tossing in a stiff breeze.

'It'll be cool out on the water,' Simon said at breakfast. 'Bring plenty of sweaters with you. You can always shed them when we drop anchor.'

Caroline had caught her hair back in a high ponytail to keep it out of the way, a young and carefree style very different from the demure way she had worn it in London. But combined with jeans it had the effect of making her look like a school-girl and certainly no match for Velma in her immaculately tailored slacks, her long black hair held in place by a sophisticated bandeau.

Giles called for them as arranged. 'I don't like the look of the weather,' he said tersely. 'It could well be blowing up for rain. I hope you're all good sailors.'

Velma slid into the front seat of the Peugeot and Caroline, holding down her newly acquired resentment, meekly climbed into the back with Simon. Giles was wearing pale blue trousers and a matching windcheater, and he

162

and Velma, tanned and casually elegant, looked like an advertisement from a glossy sailing magazine. Caroline hunched into her sweater and tried not to feel scruffy. Simon's hand closed over hers and gave it a reassuring little squeeze and she flashed him a grateful smile.

By St Luc's harbour the wind was stronger than ever, slapping their faces and tossing away their breath. Velma threaded her arm through Giles's and, heads down, they set off along the quay to where the boat was berthed, Caroline and Simon following behind. The path led out into the harbour, with boats on either side rocking and swaying as the sea slapped against them. Overhead, white clouds scudded furiously and voices were carried on the wind, shrill and disembodied as the cries of gulls. When they stopped alongside Giles's boat, it seemed only natural to find the name *La Mouette* painted on its hull. Caroline remarked on it to Simon, and at his enquiring look, explained that it meant 'Seagull'.

'Personally I'd feel safer on an albatross in this wind!' he said with a grin.

The captain was waiting at the gangplank to help them aboard. The planks were slippery from flying spray and Caroline was grateful for her plimsolls. She followed Velma on to the small deck while Giles remained talking to the man on the quay.

The boat was beautifully appointed and

163

brasswork gleamed against the white paint. Cushions and sun-loungers were stacked at one side. 'I doubt if we'll be sitting out here today,' Simon remarked ruefully. 'It'll be more a question of being strapped to the mast—if there is one!'

'Only a radio mast,' Giles answered, coming up behind them. He introduced them to the captain, Pierre, and Jacques the steward. 'Are you going to stay on deck or would you rather retire to the saloon?'

Simon turned to Caroline.

'Could I have a quick look round the boat first?' she asked Giles.

'Of course. Show her, would you, Simon? I'm going forward until we're out of harbour. Come up if you'd like to, otherwise make yourselves at home in there. Jacques will have coffee ready in a few minutes.'

He turned and made his way to the bow, followed by Velma. Simon slid open the glazed door leading to the saloon and Caroline exclaimed in admiration. A corner sofa upholstered in black and white tweed ran along the port side, with a coffee table in front of it. Beyond was a small dinette with seating for four, while a cocktail bar and television set stood against the opposite wall. The floor was covered with a charcoal grey carpet. Down the ladder she found a compact little galley complete with fridge, cooker and sink, where, as Giles had anticipated, Jacques was already

164

at work preparing coffee, and beyond it were the two cabins, each with two berths and its own small bathroom.

'The crew have a cabin forward,' Simon explained. 'It's very neat, isn't it? Everything to hand.'

The engines had started up, throbbing under their feet, and they retraced their steps to the windy deck as the boat began to move. Giles and Velma were leaning on the rail, his arm round her shoulders. Caroline took her place beside him, watching with fascination as the vessel threaded its way out of the crowded harbour. On reaching the open sea the wind veered, flinging spray in their faces, and Giles straightened, glancing down at her.

'All right?' he asked abruptly.

'Fine. She's a lovely boat.'

He nodded. 'Right, everyone. Coffee, I think. Let's hope the rain keeps off.'

They went back to the saloon and Giles switched on the radio. 'We can relax with music; Pierre'll keep his ears open for any gale warnings, though I don't think it will come to that.' He flicked a glance at Caroline. 'My apologies. I could have chosen better weather for your day out.'

'I'm enjoying it,' she said staunchly. 'There's been an awful lot of sunshine.'

'Don't complain, you'll be back in London soon enough!'

The coffee swirled around in the cups and

165

drinking it called for a steady hand.

'Do you keep the boat here all year round?' Caroline asked Giles.

'Yes, since she's registered in St Luc she just goes into winter storage.'

'And you always have the same crew?'

'They've been with me for a couple of years now. They work full-time during the season and find other employment in the winter. They're cousins and get on well together and Pierre's English is quite good, which, as you'll appreciate, was one reason why I hired him in the first place.'

Though he was addressing her pleasantly enough, Caroline noted that Giles wasn't meeting her eye. Velma, she thought despairingly, had never looked more beautiful. The chunky white sweater contrasted with the smooth line of her brown throat above it and she had a sleek, self-satisfied look about her that Caroline found hard to take. Certainly Giles seemed to be paying her more attention than usual.

Out on the deck again, he took up a position directly behind her, arms encircling her to protect her from the backlash of wind. Caroline said brightly, 'What can you see from the back?' and, holding on to the rail for support, made her way aft, loyally followed by Simon.

'You're not feeling queasy or anything, are you, love?'

166

'No,' she answered carefully, 'not anything.' Which wasn't quite true. The line of the coast was speeding by parallel to their progress, and from out here the nearness of the mountains was very noticeable, rising up behind the small resorts and inlets in majestic sweeps of rock and dense forest. After a while Giles and Velma came to join them.

'Normally I make for one of the islands and go ashore in the dinghy,' he explained. 'It's very pleasant pottering and swimming around and there are excellent restaurants on the beaches. However, it's hardly the weather for that today, so we might as well go farther afield. Let's go inside and have a drink while I look at the map.'

The saloon was warm after the coolness outside and the girls removed their sweaters. Tendrils of hair had escaped from Caroline's ponytail and were curling against her neck. Velma disappeared below to tidy herself. When she returned she joined Giles at the chart table and his arm automatically went round her. Caroline bit her lip and resolutely looked away.

'We could get to Blancheterre fairly comfortably, I think. There's a Roman temple on the hill behind, which is well worth a visit.'

He went through to the wheelhouse to have a word with Pierre. Caroline sat on the tweed sofa and reached for one of the magazines. It was all about sailing and she flicked the pages

167

without interest, trying to come to terms with the increasing hopelessness inside her. The worst part of it was wondering whether if she'd proved less intractable she would have stood a chance with Giles. Or would he merely have tired of her sooner? He seemed to be going out of his way to show his lack of interest. Perhaps this was part of his promise not to upset her.

Simon draped an arm round her neck and she had to restrain an impatient impulse to shrug him away. It was turning into a perfectly horrible day.

There was worse to come. The wind had freshened considerably when they tied up alongside at Blancheterre. It was one o'clock and Giles arranged with the crew to be back on board by five.

'That will give us time to have a leisurely lunch and then climb up to the ruin. You're not in any hurry to get back, are you?'

'No,' Velma assured him, 'we told Grandmother to expect us when she saw us.'

The wind-skimmed streets were almost empty and when they reached a restaurant they saw why. Everyone had deserted the bleakness outside in favour of the comforts of warmth and good food. They waited at the bar until a table was free, and service was very slow. But despite the excess of fresh air, Caroline was not hungry. She had a little of the *hors-d'oeuvres variés* that the others had ordered, but the large plates of *gnocchi niçois* were beyond her and she settled for a slice of *pissaladière.*

'It's just as well we allowed plenty of time,' Giles remarked when at last they finished their meal. 'It's quite a way up to the temple.'

They set off as before, he and Velma in the lead, Caroline and Simon bringing up the rear. And the oftener this happened, the more it seemed the decreed order of things.

Up the narrow winding roads, not unlike those of St Luc, and then, above the town, on to the lower scrubland of the hill, where the wind blowing straight from the sea buffeted against them with a hint of dampness in its breath.

Giles hesitated. 'I wonder if we should go on. There's no shelter up there if it starts to rain.'

'Having got this far, I'm certainly not turning back,' Velma declared. 'Anyway, I love walking in the rain.'

'Walking, perhaps, but not slithering and slipping on a grassy hillside.'

'I'll hold you up, darling!' she promised gaily, and Caroline had an unworthy urge to slap her lovely face. Grimly she hung on to Simon's hand and kept climbing, closing her mind to the tugging muscles behind her knees, the pain in her chest and the even greater pain in her heart. She'd wanted to spend the day with Giles, she reminded herself grimly, and

169

she was doing just that.

The indistinct ruins of the temple appeared on the skyline above them, reminding Caroline of that other ruin on the road to Ste Emmanuelle, where Giles had caught her against him. If only she could have that moment handed back to her, how very differently she would react.

It was as they came abreast of the ancient pillars that the rain started in earnest. Caroline pulled up the wide cowl neckline of her sweater and stuck her hands in the pockets of her jeans. She didn't care what she looked like; Giles wasn't looking at her, anyway.

'Oh boy!' Simon said.

They turned and stared back the way they had come. Sea and town were blotted out behind a curtain of driving rain and they were cut off in the wraiths of low cloud which hung over the hill.

'It's small consolation, but there's usually a magnificent view,' Giles said tightly. 'Come round the other side of this arch; it might be a bit more sheltered.'

Huddled together against the cold grey stone, they stood staring out at the desolate wind-lashed grass and eventually, accepting that the rain wasn't going to lessen for some time, set off down the hill again, their shoes squelching and sliding on the slippery ground. At least, Caroline thought, as they reached the upper part of the town again, the weather was in keeping with her mood.

'I'm glad you like walking in the rain, Velma!' Simon remarked, pushing his dripping hair back from his face.

'There's rain and rain, admittedly. Still, it's not really cold.'

'It's entirely my fault,' said Giles. 'I should never have attempted taking you up there while the weather was so uncertain.'

Jacques and Pierre, enviably dry, were waiting with towels to dry off the worst of the rain.

'I keep a few clothes in the cabin,' Giles informed them, 'but I doubt if there's anything that would do for you girls. Still, the first thing is to take off those wet things, even if you have to wrap yourselves in blankets while they dry.'

They went below to the main cabin and he opened one of the hanging lockers, taking out shorts, slacks and a couple of sweaters. 'Ah, you're in luck!' he said over his shoulder. 'There's an old bathrobe here which is better than nothing, and—'

He broke off and Velma reached past him and drew out a black chiffon negligee. 'Well, well, look what I've found! I wondered what had happened to it!'

'It must have been there since last year.' Giles's voice was clipped.

'Too long, certainly.'

He thrust the towelling robe into Caroline's arms. 'You two make use of this cabin; Simon

171

and I will use the other. Have a hot shower if you're chilled.'

The door closed behind the men and Velma laughed softly. 'Poor darling, he was quite embarrassed!' She stripped off her clothes and padded into the bathroom. Caroline rubbed herself vigorously with the towel and slipped into the voluminous folds of Giles's robe. It smelled of salt and sand and sun-tan lotion. She dragged the ponytail toggle from her hair with difficulty, squeezed out the surplus moisture and towelled it dry. Fortunately she had a hairbrush in her handbag.

Behind the closed door of the little bathroom Velma was singing softly above the rushing water. Caroline had no intention of waiting for her to emerge in the filmy negligee. She went back up to the saloon. Giles, over by the table, turned at her approach.

'There's some hot tea, if you'd like it.'

'I would, thank you.' She went across and took the mug he held out, clasping her hands round it.

'I'm really very sorry about all this. You'll wish you hadn't agreed to come.'

'Not at all. I've never been on a boat like this before, and anyway—'

'And I doubt if you will again, given the choice.'

'I'm sure it's usually very different. Giles, I wanted to—'

'Drink your tea while it's hot.'

172

She said quietly, 'Please let me speak.'

He eyed her warily. 'Well?'

'I wanted to say that I—understand now. About my father. I hadn't really—'

'And I understand too, Caroline. It's hardly surprising you feel as you do, but at least the matter is cleared up now.'

'Is it?' she asked numbly.

He looked at her for a moment, hair curling round her face in still-damp tendrils, eyes large over the rim of the mug she held in both hands. His mouth tightened and he said evenly, 'Of course. I'm only sorry you didn't tell me before. My frequent appearances at the villa must have been very distressing for you in the circumstances. Had I known, of course I'd have stayed away.'

'But I don't want you to go on thinking—'

'I shan't think about it any more, and I hope you won't, either. We can put the whole thing behind us now. Ah, here's Simon. Have some tea to warm you up.'

Caroline took a gulp of the hot liquid, welcoming the pain as it scorched down her throat. Well, that was clear enough. He simply wanted to forget her, together with all the trouble she'd caused him over the last two months.

The boat had left its moorings and she stood at the window looking out as they moved into the open sea and the lights of Blancheterre receded into the distance. The heavy rain was contributing to a premature darkness and as she turned away Giles, with a brisk, 'Let's shut it out now', drew the curtains.

Velma looked disturbingly seductive, barefoot and in her negligee. She curled like a cat in the corner of the sofa. Giles's sweater and shorts were a little too big for Simon, giving him the appearance of a small boy in his father's clothes.

'We're a motley crew, I must say!' he commented, rolling up the sleeves.

'At least we're dry,' Giles said shortly. He switched on the radio. 'Anyone like anything to eat? Fruit, biscuits?'

They shook their heads and he sat down next to Velma. 'If Tom and Richard were here, they'd be organising a game of bridge by now. Would anyone like to play?'

'I'm perfectly happy just relaxing,' Velma murmured, nestling against him.

Caroline hastily retrieved the magazine she had looked through earlier. There were so many things she didn't want to think about— Giles's curt dismissal, the missed opportunities she'd had, Velma's negligee and the implications behind it. Yet the other girl was a much more suitable companion for Giles than she could ever be—self-possessed, glamorous, sophisticated.

Holding the magazine as a cover, she watched Giles from beneath her lashes, trying to imprint every detail of him in her memory in case she never saw him again. The possibility, too enormous to grasp, was in fact quite a likely one. This outing was simply the fulfilment of an earlier promise. He'd asked yesterday if she still wanted to come, no doubt hoping she wouldn't, and after what he'd just said it was more than probable that he'd stay away from the villa during the last few days of her stay there.

He was talking quietly to Velma, his dark head bent to hers. Caroline's eyes traced the line of nose and brow, the slight groove in his cheek, the firm mouth whose strength and passion had so roused her. One arm was lying along the back of the sofa, the hairs on it bleached golden by the sun, and his open shirt exposed the smooth brown skin of chest and throat.

Yet it was not only his outward appearance that attracted her. While her physical response had been immediate, she hadn't realised that behind the screen of antagonism her mind had been making its own evaluation. Only now the barrier was removed could she discover, too late, how much about Giles appealed to her: his quick wit and sense of humour; his ideas on contemporary issues and the clarity with which he expressed them; his air of easy authority, the almost unconscious assumption of command. And she was warmed by his obvious fondness for Adeline and the deference which he accorded her. All these facets combined

175

with his external attraction went to make up the man she loved.

Wasn't it George Bernard Shaw who had described love as simply a gross exaggeration of the difference between one person and everyone else? Certainly, Giles was like no one she had ever known, and the memories of her times with him returned to haunt her, accompanied as they were by a host of regretful 'if onlys'.

From the radio came the lilting strains of *La Vie en rose*, and almost unconsciously she began to hum it under her breath.

'Do you know the words?' Simon asked her.

'Yes; it's one of my favourites.'

'Sing it, then.'

'Oh no, I—'

'Go on, Caroline,' Velma urged. 'Sing it. We'd like to hear.'

Softly she began: ' *"Quand il me prend dans ses bras"* ' Her low, sweet voice was admirably suited to the plaintive melody and the three of them sat motionless, listening. The achingly sweet words caught at her throat and it was a wonder to her that she could sing at all.

'That was lovely, Caro,' said Simon as she came to an end. 'What exactly does it mean?'

'There was an English version,' Velma put in, 'but I seem to remember they changed the meaning completely.'

'Well, Caroline?' Giles challenged her. 'You're the one for impromptu translations.

176

Let's have it in English.'

Haltingly she started to translate, pausing now and then to prompt herself with the French words: 'When he takes me in his arms, he talks to me very softly and I see life all—rosy. He speaks words of love, everyday words, and it does something to me. He has come into my heart, a part of happiness of which I know the cause. It's him for me, me for him, all our lives. He has told me so, has promised it's for always, and as soon as I catch sight of him, I feel my heart beating inside me.'

She stumbled to a halt, the blood drumming in her ears. No one spoke and she said to break the silence, 'I'm afraid it was a very literal translation. It sounds much better in French.'

Simon took her hand. 'It was beautiful.'

'It's made me feel quite romantic,' Velma murmured, and added as Giles sat unmoving, 'and there was a time, my love, when I didn't have to prompt you like that!'

He dragged his eyes away from Caroline's bent head. 'Is that a challenge?'

'Most definitely!'

'You complained before, didn't you, that I wasn't very good company this year. You're right, Velma. I've been in danger of taking myself too seriously. No more, I promise.' His hand moved from the back of the seat behind her, twining round the long black hair and tilting her head back till her face was only inches away from his. Unable to look away, Caroline's straining eyes watched as his mouth closed on Velma's and her hand slipped inside his open shirt, moving caressingly over his skin.

Beside her Simon murmured, 'If you can't beat 'em, join 'em!' and she felt his feather-light lips on hers. Briefly panic enveloped her. Giles and Velma's embrace made her physically sick and at the almost ludicrous comparison of Simon's kiss, she suddenly wanted to scream aloud her pain and frustration.

But immediately she was drenched in self-hatred. It wasn't Simon's fault that she'd made a fool of herself over Giles. He at least loved her, wanted to marry her. Dear, kind, gentle Simon! He deserved more than she was able to give him. In a hazy attempt to make up for her shortcomings, she slid an arm round his neck, holding him closer and at once despairingly aware of his partial withdrawal. Not pressing him, she nevertheless held him close until she knew from the movements at the other end of the sofa that Giles and Velma had looked up and seen them. She heard Velma say softly, 'Shall we go below?'

And Giles's uneven: 'I think not.'

Only then did she loosen her clasp of Simon's neck and as he moved back she looked challengingly across to see Giles staring at her. He stood up and moved to the cocktail

178

bar. 'I think we could do with a drink.'

Velma was lounging back in her corner. The negligee had parted slightly to expose the white mound of the top of her breast below the line of sunburn. 'Brandy sour for me, darling.'

Simon was still holding tightly to Caroline's hand. Or rather, she discovered, it was she who was gripping his. She made a conscious effort to unflex her fingers and he smiled at her a little shyly. She looked away from him to find Giles in front of her, holding out a glass, and raised her eyes to his.

'Thank you.'

The radio, which had been responsible for so much, was still playing sentimental music. Giles switched it off without a word. Caroline's hands and face were burning. She wished she could go out on deck, away from all three of them, but it was still raining and she was hampered by the overlarge bathrobe.

Jacques came out of the wheelhouse where he'd been sitting with Pierre.

'I regret the clothes are still wet, *monsieur.*'

'I don't doubt it. Never mind, we'll have to go ashore as we are. Fortunately it's almost dark and the car isn't far away.'

'Very good, *monsieur.* Is there anything I can get for you?'

'No, thank you, Jacques. I've seen to the drinks myself.'

He withdrew and they sat in suddenly

179

awkward silence, emphasised by the absence of the radio background. It was a relief to all of them when *La Mouette* entered the harbour at St Luc and dropped anchor in her own moorings. Jacques handed over their damp, neatly folded clothes and they stumbled out into the windy darkness. The rain had stopped at last. Caroline clung to Simon with one hand, clasping the robe round her with the other. Then they were in the car and moments later had stopped at the villa gates. She murmured conventional thanks to Giles and hurried thankfully away from him down the drive.

When she reached her room she found to her surprise that it was only eight o'clock. It felt like midnight. She had a very hot bath and washed her hair, chose her prettiest dress and made up carefully. She was becoming quite good, she reflected, at not thinking about things.

Simon was alone in the salon when she went down. He pulled her gently against him and kissed her cheek. 'Recovered from your unnerving experience?'

'Just about.'

Velma came running lightly down the stairs. 'Simon. I'm having dinner with Giles at his villa. I rather doubt that I shall be back tonight, so cover for me, will you? You know how old-fashioned Grandmother is.'

As old-fashioned as I am, Caroline thought achingly, remembering Giles's urgent request

180

at Ste Emmanuelle, and the effort it had cost her to refuse him. Obviously Velma would have had no such scruples.

'You'd better be back in time for breakfast,' Simon advised. He looked thoughtfully after her as she hurried out of the front door. 'I don't know what to make of those two. They were very lovey-dovey today, but it didn't seem to ring quite true, on Giles's part anyway.'

'I can't think what else he could have done to convince you,' Caroline retorted brittly.

Simon smiled. 'I'm probably imagining things, but as I said before, he's an odd bloke. Perhaps she's wearing him down at last.'

Humphrey Betts had returned to London during their absence and on the spur of the moment his wife had accompanied him, which meant there were only three of them for dinner.

'What did you think of the boat, Caroline?' Adeline enquired.

'Very plush. On a good day, when you can swim and sunbathe, it must be a lovely way of spending the time. As it was, it was somewhat—claustrophobic.'

'I was expecting Giles to come back with you for dinner.'

'He and Velma probably wanted to be alone,' Simon suggested.

Adeline said, 'You're not making a very good impression on that plate, Caroline.'

'I'm sorry.' She laid down her knife and

fork. 'I'm really not hungry at all.'

'But you hardly had any lunch either,' Simon objected.

'I'm probably slightly off-colour. Perhaps the motion of the boat.' She looked pleadingly at her employer. 'Would you excuse me if I went straight to bed?' Her control was rapidly running out and she saw the old eyes soften as Adeline nodded.

'Of course, child. Off you go. It will be better in the morning.'

Without bothering to analyse the rather enigmatic remark, Caroline left them and hurried to the blissful privacy of her room.

CHAPTER TEN

As Simon had advised, Velma was at the breakfast table the next morning, but only to inform her grandmother that she and Giles were going to Ste Maxime to stay with friends for a couple of nights.

'You don't mind, do you, Grandmother? I'll be back on Wednesday, a full week before you go home.'

'Before *I* do? Aren't you coming with us?'

'I'm not sure.' Velma toyed with her knife.

'It depends on Giles, I suppose,' said Adeline resignedly.

'To some extent, yes.'

'Well, I'm sorry you won't be here this evening. I've invited the Varleys for dinner.'

Velma smiled. 'I'm not going to pretend I'm sorry to miss them.'

'They're a very nice family,' her grandmother retorted severely. 'Since I couldn't go over with the rest of you on Saturday, I arranged for them to come here instead.'

'Simon will get a double dose!' Velma said mischievously. 'But I don't suppose he'll object, and I'm quite sure Amy won't!'

Ignoring her, Adeline turned to Caroline. 'We've known them for years. Jane Varley was at school with Lydia. However—' she folded her napkin—'I shall put them out of my mind until this evening. We're on the last chapter of the book now and I'm determined to finish it before we go home.'

Velma said comfortably, 'Then you'll be glad to have me out of the way! Is Mother coming back for Jeremy's party?'

'She wasn't sure. If she does, she'll stay on for a while when I leave, but I think your father may well talk her out of it. He's been on his own long enough. He's not as young as he was. If you're ready, Caroline, let's retire to the study, shall we?'

In silence Caroline followed her across the hall. The relief in the knowledge that she wouldn't see Giles for at least a couple of days was offset by the fact that he'd be spending them with Velma. But that, she reminded herself, was nothing to do with her. She could have returned his bathrobe via Velma, but she intended to wash it first, refusing to accept the fact that she didn't want to part with it.

Monday was a day Adeline often found difficult after the interruption of the weekend and it usually took the whole morning before she was back in the swing of the book again. This week, however, she had apparently been working alone the previous day and was able to get down to work straightaway. It was going so well that it seemed a shame to break off at lunch time, and Caroline suggested that unless Mrs Stevens wanted her usual rest, they should continue working. For herself she was only too thankful to have the hours usefully occupied and her mind kept busy. Consequently by the time they stopped work at four-thirty, the end of the book was in sight.

'That's splendid, Caroline!' Adeline exclaimed jubilantly. 'We'll finish it this week and it will be ready to hand over to my agent as soon as we return to London.'

Caroline paused in the act of putting the cover on her typewriter. 'I suppose you won't want me any more then?'

'Of course I shall, dear, but first you'll be free to have a nice long holiday—with pay, of course. By September I shall start getting restless again and ready to start on something else. As I explained, this book had dragged on far longer than it should, due to the interruption of your predecessor leaving. So you can relax for the rest of the summer and report for duty at the beginning of September.' She smiled. 'Which doesn't, of course, mean that I shan't be delighted to see you socially during that time, if you're in London. Now, off you go, child. The Varleys will be arriving about seven, so I'll expect you downstairs then.'

Simon was sitting alone on the terrace and she went out to join him. She was mentally tired after such a prolonged and intensive bout of Adeline's creativity and it was pleasant to relax next to Simon with closed eyes. This time yesterday they'd been stumbling down the hillside in the rain. Her hands tightened on the armrests and before she could stop herself she wondered what Giles and Velma were doing at this moment.

It was no good, she thought wearily. It seemed she was split in half, part of her with Giles and only a part remaining. She had to put an end to this fragmented existence, and the best way would be by marrying Simon. She was surprised to find that her subconscious had apparently already accepted this conclusion, for as it reached the conscious level she felt no surprise. He was never cruel or unpredictable or sarcastic and she was genuinely fond of him. She recalled that when they first arrived at the villa she had assumed they would eventually marry. She had only prevaricated because in her innocence she was afraid she might be missing something, wanted to experience the full passion of love.

A shudder rippled over her. Well, she had done just that. She knew now what it was to be kissed by a man who desired her, and to desire him in return. She knew without any doubt what love felt like, and the answer was unmitigated despair and misery, an aching, yearning void which could never be filled. So now she would be only too grateful to accept Simon's offer of tenderness, affection and companionship. She was sure she could make him happy, and in time it was even possible she might be happy again herself.

She reached out a hand and he took it at once.

'What is it, sweetheart?'

'Nothing, really. I'm just—glad you're there.'

He said, as Giles had once said, 'Oh, Caroline!' and her teeth fastened in her lip. There were bound to be such occasions, she told herself shakily. Time would take care of most of them. In the meantime, when the right moment offered, she would let him know that she was now ready to accept his proposal.

Not this evening, though. This evening the Varleys were coming to dinner, and she was curious to see this girl who idolised Simon so much.

Her first sight of Amy was a shock. It was like looking into a mirror of three months ago—the same pale, oval face, large eyes, quiet manner. On more detailed inspection, Amy was younger and fairer than herself. Her pale hair hung from a centre parting, straight and shining, and her eyes were grey rather than the tawny-gold of Caroline's own. She wore a high-necked 'little girl' dress in baby blue, with a nipped-in waist and full skirt, and by contrast Caroline's coffee lace appeared the last word in sophistication.

Ironic that only yesterday she had herself felt gauche beside Velma's sleek elegance. But yesterday was a closed subject, behind her now, as Giles had said.

Giles! The sharp pain again, taking her unawares. With a caught breath she recovered her balance and went forward to meet Amy's parents. They were, as Adeline had said, a pleasant couple in their late forties. Jane was attractive and vivacious, chatting incessantly, and Caroline began to perceive one possible reason for her daughter's shyness. Michael Varley was prematurely grey, but his thick wavy hair was striking against the bronzed youthfulness of his face. Caroline liked him instantly. Quieter than his wife, he nevertheless had a dry sense of humour which appealed to her.

Out of the corner of her eye as she chatted to him, she saw that Simon had joined Amy on the sofa and the girl's pale face was flushed with pleasure. She looked hastily away to catch Michael's eyes assessingly on her. Did he consider her a threat to his daughter's happiness? Oh, *damn* love! Caroline thought suddenly. It seemed it always had to hurt someone.

As so often happened at the villa, an unexpected ring at the door heralded the arrival of more friends who, secure in the assured welcome, 'just happened' to drop in as they were passing. They were of course included in the invitation to dinner, and Caroline marvelled yet again at the resources of Madame Perrier who took these upheavals so calmly in her stride. On this occasion the uninvited guests were Val Parkes, her parents and her fiancé, whom Caroline knew quite well, and their presence was welcome in that it made a more diffuse gathering than the concentration of the Varleys. And perhaps, she thought, she wouldn't be subjected to quite so much attention from Mr Varley.

'Where's Velma?' Val asked Caroline. 'Aren't she and Giles in for dinner?'

'They've gone to some friends at Ste Maxime,' Caroline replied steadily.

'Ruth and David? Pity—we could have gone too if we'd known. Not,' she added hastily, 'that it isn't lovely to be here! I haven't seen the Varleys for ages. Poor Amy still hasn't got over Simon, has she? It's been going on for ages, but at least this year he's actually noticed her.' She stopped, colour flooding her face. 'It seems to be my evening for *faux pas*! I only meant—'

'I know what you meant,' Caroline assured her, but she felt a small flicker of fear. Surely, having come to a decision about Simon, she wasn't about to lose him too? As Velma had astutely observed, this girl was so like herself when Simon had first been attracted to her. And what was it he'd said? 'To me you were lovelier when you were pale and quiet and desperate.'

'All the same,' she added to Val, 'I think I'll go and find out what they're talking about!'

Simon looked up as she approached and rose to his feet. 'Come and join us, sweetheart. Amy was telling me about a book she's reading.'

The endearment was balm to Caroline's uncertain heart, but she had been looking at the girl and saw the flash of anxiety in her eyes. She said out of a vast pity, 'Oh? Who's it by?'

Amy replied and started to outline the plot and Caroline wondered incredulously if she regarded herself as she thought of Velma—a threat to well-being, a predatory, smiling enemy.

They went down the steps to the dining-room. Although for the last month they'd been eating out on the terrace, the remnants of yesterday's strong wind made this undesirable tonight. Simon was seated at one end of the table, with Caroline and Amy opposite each other on either side of him. Mr Parkes was on Caroline's left. He was a jolly man and kept her laughing. For the first time in two days she was able to do justice to a meal, and felt all the better for it. On the other hand, she couldn't help noticing that across the table Amy Varley ate very little.

Simon, flushed with a little more wine than he was used to, and perhaps also by the attention of the girls on either side of him, looked quite handsome, Caroline thought fondly. His fair skin, which had reddened painfully when first exposed to the sun, had toned down to an acceptable light tan and his blue eyes as always were warm and honest. No wonder poor little Amy loved him; she almost did herself, though a large proportion of what she felt was gratitude for his own devotion.

When the evening was over, Simon walked to the gate with the visitors and Caroline waited on the terrace for his return, leaning on the parapet and staring down the shadowed garden. She didn't turn as he came back and slipped an arm round her waist.

'You're fond of Amy, aren't you?'

'Oh, she's a nice little thing. She brings out all my protective instincts, like you used to.'

'Used to?'

'Well, look at you, sweetie. You hardly need protecting now, do you? Except from Giles, of

190

course. I do wish you'd told me about your father, Caro.'

'What difference would it have made?'

'I could have kept Giles out of your way, for a start. You were always on edge with him, but I never realised there was such good reason for it. And quite apart from that—well, it would have been a sign of trust.'

She slipped an arm round his neck. 'It was nothing to do with lack of trust,' she said gently. 'When I first met you in London it was all too recent and I couldn't bear to talk about it. Afterwards, not having mentioned it, it became progressively harder to, and of course when we arrived here and I found you actually knew Giles, it would have been too awkward for words to have blurted everything out. After all, you said he was a friend of the family and a constant visitor. I was very thankful I *hadn't* mentioned Daddy to any of you.'

'Yes, I can see that. I was just sorry that in the end you told Giles before me.'

'He insisted on knowing,' she said levelly.

'Why?'

'I suppose he resented my attitude. With reason.'

'It must have been a change for him. Most women seem to find him attractive, though according to Grandmother he doesn't often get involved himself. But don't let's waste time talking about Giles.' He pulled her closer and began to kiss her gently—her face, her closed eyelids, her lips. This time she made no attempt to intensify the embrace, and after a moment he said softly, 'You seem so far away.'

'When I try to come closer, you move away.' She hadn't meant to say that, and felt his embarrassment.

'Actually, I was speaking metaphorically.'

'You don't like to be too close physically, do you?'

'I think it's rather—asking for trouble.' He moved slightly. 'You must think me a fool.'

'No!' she said sharply. 'Oh Simon, no—I don't. I'm the one who's inconsistent, not you.' She held him tightly, pressing against him but more as if he were an elder brother than a lover. He seemed to recognise the difference, and his arms tightened round her.

'There, there, Caro. It's all right, love. It's all right.'

'I'm not surprised you don't understand me.' Her voice was muffled against his shoulder. 'I don't understand myself.'

'It doesn't matter, love. Really.' He kissed her hair. 'You're overtired, that's the trouble. That long session with Grandmother exhausted you. You'll feel better tomorrow.'

But would she? Would she ever?

She extricated herself gently, reached up and kissed his mouth. 'Goodnight, Simon.'

'Goodnight, my darling.'

But was she only his darling, she wondered as she undressed, when she was miserable and unsure of herself? Or, more pertinently, was that the only time she turned to him?

The next morning work continued satisfactorily on the book, and it was obvious they would finish it the following day.

'We shan't work right through today,' Adeline announced. 'I need my afternoon rest in this heat. Thank goodness we'll be home next week. I find it very tiring here now.'

Simon was in for lunch, and after the meal he and Caroline went down to the pool. Oranges and lemons glowed exotically among their dark leaves and the pine trees stood dull and dusty in the heat. Simon rigged up an umbrella, angling it so that its shadow didn't fall over Caroline.

'No point in having finally built up a tan, only to return home all blistered! It's all right for you, you just soak it in, turning an ever more gorgeous colour!'

'I want to make the most of this last week,' explained Caroline. 'There's no guarantee of the weather at home!'

'It seems odd to think that now all the exams are over, I shan't have another long holiday till I'm about sixty-five!'

'When do you start your job?' she asked.

'Not till the middle of September.'

'But you're coming back with us next week?'

'Yes. I'm not really a sun-worshipper and it would seem very empty here without you.'

Caroline was disconcerted to find herself

wondering when the Varleys were returning home. 'Simon—'

'Um?'

Her fingernails were biting into the palms of her hands. 'I don't know how to say this.'

He turned on to his front, so that he was right alongside her, looking down into her face. 'Say what?'

'Do you still want to marry me?'

There was a short silence. Then he said, 'Of course.'

'You've never mentioned it since that first evening.'

'You said you wanted time.'

'But didn't you ever wonder?'

'I can be patient, Caro. Sometimes, perhaps, too patient.' He paused. 'Have you come to a decision?'

She said in a rush, 'I think I'd like to marry you, if you still want me to.' She looked up at him almost fearfully and he smiled, one finger gently tracing her nose and mouth.

'Then that's fine.'

She said with difficulty, 'You don't have to feel bound. I mean, if you've changed your mind—'

'What interests me is why you've changed yours. I'd have said we've grown apart rather than closer in the time we've been here. I was afraid you'd—outgrown me.'

She reached up and caught his hand, holding it against her face. 'On the contrary,

I've discovered how valuable the things you offered are.'

'Would it be out of place to ask if you love me?' said Simon.

'I told you before that I did.'

' "In a way." Yes, I remember.'

'And you said—you'd enough for both of us.'

'I remember that, too. And this is what you really want?'

'Yes. I can't think why I waited so long. It's a wonderful, safe feeling, knowing someone loves you.'

'You make me feel like an insurance company. "Wrap the warmth of our protection all around you!" That kind of thing. But I doubt if anyone actually loves insurance companies!'

Her eyes filled with tears and Simon exclaimed, 'Oh, Caro love, I was only joking! If that's what you want, O.K. I offered you your own terms before, and it still holds. The only thing that worries me is that you've changed so much I'm no longer sure I can give you what you want.'

She said brokenly, 'I only want what you can give me.'

He moved slightly closer and bent his head to kiss her. Caroline could feel the length of his bare leg against hers and it meant nothing. Her body didn't even quiver in response. But she'd had enough of that and she would never do anything to cause Simon pain or doubt about offering her his love.

'You're so beautiful,' he said softly. He rested his head on her breast and her fingers automatically caressed his hair. Nothing, she thought blankly. Absolutely nothing. Perhaps in time some faint response would grow, and that would be enough. It was tenderness and understanding she wanted, not the wild, selfish passion she'd experienced with Giles.

'Grandmother will be pleased,' Simon said after a while, and she wondered what thoughts he'd been pursuing while she was engrossed in her own.

'But not your parents.'

'Oh, I don't know. They were quite impressed to learn who your father was.'

So that made her acceptable after all. *Tant mieux.*

'Have you any relations to inform?'

'No one.'

'Poor little Caroline!'

She said suddenly, 'Simon, it is enough, isn't it? What I'm offering you?'

'It is for me, sweetheart, as long as you're happy. I'm afraid I'm not the sweep-them-off-their-feet type, but you don't need telling that.' He gave a short laugh. 'Perhaps, we'll start the fashion, and Velma and Giles will follow suit.' He raised his head and looked into her face. 'Caro—'

'Yes?' She held her breath. What was he

196

going to ask? Something, she couldn't answer?

'It doesn't matter. It feels odd to be engaged, doesn't it? I suppose we are engaged?'

'I suppose so.' Certainly it wasn't the remotest bit as she'd dreamed it would be, but dreams and real life were two different things, opposite sides of the coin. Fact and fancy, romance and common sense. She was aching all over with the effort of holding back her tears.

'I'm too hot!' she said unsteadily. 'I'm going in for a swim.' And she jumped into the pool, the silken rift of the water parting to admit her and closing again over her head. Rapidly she swam under the surface to the far side of the pool and came up to find Simon beside her. The sudden release from the tension that had been between them exploded into energy. They raced each other backwards and forwards down the pool, laughing and gasping and wiping the water out of their eyes, and Simon caught her wet body against his and kissed her firmly. Perhaps it would be all right after all.

They told Adeline when they met in the salon before dinner.

'Well, this is quite a surprise, I must say! When was it all arranged?'

'I asked Caro ages ago, when we first arrived here.'

'And she's only just made up her mind?'

Caroline said lightly, 'I'm the cautious type!'

'So I'm the first to be told? I'm very honoured.' Adeline went to Caroline and kissed her warmly on the cheek. 'I hope you'll be very, very happy, my dear.'

'Thank you.' *Don't cry!* she thought fiercely. Brides might be allowed to, but fiancées never.

'Simon, go and ask Gaston to find us a bottle of champagne. This calls for a celebration.'

Caroline walked to the window. Behind her, she heard Adeline say quietly, 'This isn't the news I was expecting, Caroline. Are you sure you know what you're doing?'

'I think so.'

'What about Giles? Surely you don't deny there's something between you?'

'There's nothing, Mrs Stevens. Nothing.' Her voice shook.

Adeline said gently, 'You know your own mind, of course, but don't forget that I know Giles. I've never seen him like this before. He can't keep his eyes off you.'

Caroline found she was gripping the curtain, crumpling and squeezing the heavy material in her hand. When she could speak, she said, 'He finds me attractive, but against his will. It's all been rather—difficult.'

'I don't want Simon hurt.'

'Nor do I.'

'On the other hand, I don't like to see you so unhappy. This isn't how it should be.'

198

'It'll be all right. I know it will.'

'That's fine, then. We'll say no more about it.'

During dinner, it was Adeline who kept the conversational ball in play, and after ascertaining that they had no immediate wedding plans, the talk turned quite naturally away from the engagement, centring on the happenings at the villa and the novel as it did every evening. Once, Caroline even caught herself wondering why they were drinking champagne. As it happened, both she and Simon were grateful for the normality. The fact of their engagement had assumed overwhelming proportions and they were both conscious of taking an involuntary step backwards. They needed time to come to terms with it.

'Jeremy's party on Saturday will be an appropriate end-of-season occasion, as far as we're concerned,' Adeline was saying. 'It seems a long time since our housewarming.'

A long time since those unknown arms had come round her in the dark, and she had learned for the first time the intoxicating sensations her body could enjoy.

'I believe a few Hollywood moguls will be there, which can't be a bad thing!' Adeline glanced at their abstracted faces. 'A word of caution, my dears. There must be no announcement of the engagement until Lydia and Humphrey have been told. Till then, we

199

must keep it in the family.'

Which, to Adeline, included Giles. At least poor little Amy would be granted a postponement of heartache.

When Adeline retired to bed, Simon and Caroline sat close together on the sofa watching a dubbed Western on television. There was something ludicrous in hearing John Wayne speak French with no trace of an accent.

'Comes to something when I need subtitles to watch a Western!' Simon grumbled humorously.

Caroline was merely relieved that among all the gun-slinging and arrow-shooting there was no hint of romance. She couldn't have borne to watch a love story tonight.

'When's Velma expected back?' she asked.

'In time for dinner, she said.'

'She always seems to gauge her return by meals! In time for dinner, or in time for breakfast.'

'Actually, she didn't stay the night with Giles on Sunday,' said Simon. 'I met her on the stairs when I came down for a glass of water. It was only about twelve.'

'Oh.' Ridiculous to feel a sudden lift of the heart.

'I told you I thought there was something slightly off-key.'

'They went away together the next day.'

'To stay with friends. That's different,

especially when it's Ruth and David. She's a vicar's daughter and has very definite ideas of the proprieties. There's never any hanky-panky in her house.'

'Oh,' Caroline said again, weakly. And all the time she'd been imagining—Not, of course, that anything Giles and Velma did was any concern of hers.

He can't keep his eyes off you.

I shan't think about it any more.

She reached up suddenly to kiss Simon's cheek and he patted her shoulder absent-mindedly, eyes still on the screen. Surely it was unusual to spend one's engagement evening watching a film on television—and in French, at that. Perhaps it was symbolic: their life together would be placid and contented. Not too much champagne and excitement, plenty of evenings sitting companionably watching television. It sounded like a Darby and Joan club.

'I think I'll go to bed, Simon. You stay, if you want to see the end of the film.'

'All right, love.' He held his face up for her to kiss. 'Sleep well.'

She turned by the pillar for a final look, but the Indians had surrounded the wagon-train and he was following their every move. Caroline went to bed.

CHAPTER ELEVEN

Caroline awoke the next morning with two facts looming large in her head. She was engaged to Simon, and today Giles would learn of it. She tested them one against the other, uneasily wondering if she was seeking some form of revenge in proclaiming to Giles that she was going to marry Simon. Certainly she was anxious to see his reaction, though there was no reason to think he'd react at all. It had been a very low-key engagement all round. She herself had been unable to summon up any excitement, and extremes of emotion seemed to be out of Simon's psychological range.

'How's the bride-to-be this morning?' Adeline enquired as she entered the study.

'Very well, thank you.'

'Ready to finish the *magnum opus*?'

'Of course.'

'Good. Then let's get straight down to it.'

The involved intricacies of the final chapter kept them occupied through the lunch hour and it was two-thirty before all the threads were joined together and the novel shown to be one satisfying whole.

'It's marvellous!' Caroline exclaimed, flipping her notebook shut. 'I've enjoyed every minute of it!'

'Bless you, dear. Let's hope for a similar reaction elsewhere. I'm pleased with it, I have to admit, and I'm extremely grateful for all the help you gave me on the research and so on. It's a great boon to be able to hand over all that side of it and know it will be done thoroughly. Fond as I was of Mary, I have to admit she was hopeless in a reference library. I was constantly coming on vital facts that she'd overlooked. Now, once all this is typed up you'll be free to spend the last few days here with Simon. Where is he, by the way?'

'He had a long-standing arrangement to go water-skiing with Steve.'

'Oh yes, of course. Well, I'll go up to my room now. I'll see you at dinner; it will have to be champagne again.'

The afternoon had clouded over and although it was very hot, there was little point in trying to sunbathe. Had it not been for Jeremy Tait's party, they would have been returning home today. Caroline very much wished they were. She would be glad when the next week was over. She and Simon had come together in London in the first place, and when they returned there, away from all the disturbing associations of the Côte d'Azur, she was sure they would become close again. Or so she told herself.

She felt restless, at a loose end. She didn't want to swim, couldn't be bothered to catch the bus to St Luc. She would have been happy to start typing out the last chapter, but Mrs Stevens' room was directly above the study and the noise would have disturbed her.

She went to the shelf of paperbacks, selected one and curled up with it in a corner of the sofa.

Slowly the afternoon passed. She wondered what time Simon would get back. They'd only seen each other briefly at breakfast and she suspected that he was glad rather than otherwise to have the water-skiing date with Steve. Oh, please make everything be all right!

She snapped the book shut, replaced it on the shelf and went upstairs. She would need all the self-confidence she could command this evening, which meant knowing that she looked her best. She took out a natural-coloured raw silk dress she had bought the week before. Its dull sheen was lit by the burnished gold of her hair and skin and she knew it flattered her. Her face, soft and glowing, did not need make-up, but she touched her lips with soft coral and hung the gold chain round her neck.

There! she thought, surveying herself critically in the glass. The picture of a radiant fiancée! And as her lip trembled she hastily turned away.

Simon was in the salon when she went down. He turned and she saw the hesitant admiration on his face. Then he came over and kissed her.

'Had a good day, sweetheart?'

'We finished the book.'

'Good. Grandmother will be relieved about that.'

'How was the skiing?' asked Caroline.

'Great. Only went under three times!'

They were talking like strangers, Caroline thought with a touch of fear. There was the sound of footsteps on the terrace and Velma came into the room with Giles behind her. And at the sight of him, all Caroline's defences crumbled. Her hand tightened on Simon's arm.

'Hello, you two. Lord, it's close out there. We drove back with all the windows open, but even the draught was hot.'

'How are the Sinclairs?' asked Simon.

'Fine. Ruth's going to have a baby—did you know?' Velma didn't wait for his reply. 'And David's been made a partner in his firm. He's very full of it.'

'Good for him.' Simon drew Caroline with him to the sofa. Giles was still standing just inside the windows.

'And what wild orgies have been going on here while we've been away?' Velma flung herself into a chair and kicked off her shoes. It occurred to Caroline that she was on edge. This constant chatter was unlike her.

Simon said carefully, 'Well, Grandmother finished her book.'

'Thank heaven for that! Now we can all relax! What's it like, Caroline?'

205

'Excellent. One of her best, I think.'

'Let's hope Hollywood will do its stuff. And how did the evening with the Varleys go?'

There was a brief pause. Simon had come to her rescue before; now it was time for her to return the favour.

'Everyone seemed to enjoy it. The Parkes were here too. They were sorry to miss you.'

'Good evening, everyone.' Adeline Stevens came into the room and Giles moved forward and kissed her cheek.

'I believe congratulations are in order.'

'Indeed. All round!'

'All round?'

Adeline looked at Simon and Caroline, then back at Giles. 'Haven't you heard the news?'

'That you've finished your book? That's what I was referring to.'

'But Simon and Caroline have something to celebrate too.' She waited a moment, and when neither of them spoke, finished: 'They became engaged yesterday.'

There was a short, electric silence, broken by a laugh from Velma. 'Well, well, little brother! You have been busy!'

Fearfully Caroline looked up at Giles. He had been staring down at her, but now he moved, holding out his hand to Simon.

'My congratulations to you both.' His eyes flickered briefly back to Caroline.

'Mine too, of course.' Velma came over and kissed them both. 'The best of luck!'

Adeline said, 'No one outside this room is to know about it until your parents have been told.'

'So they can't announce it at Jeremy's?'

'Certainly not, it would be most improper, so please don't refer to it when anyone else is present.'

'Which reminds me, Grandmother: we saw Paul and Felicity last night when we went out for drinks. They said to tell you they hope to drop in this evening, but it won't be till after dinner. They're treating themselves to *bouillabaisse*, *chez* Candide.'

Caroline's hand clenched spasmodically as her mental censor clanged into place.

'I'll be delighted to see them.' Adeline looked across at Giles, 'You're somewhat quiet this evening.'

'With respect, I haven't had the chance to be otherwise!'

'True. Take it now, or are you exhausted after all your gallivanting? You can't have had time to do any work since I last saw you.'

'No, unlike you I don't find it easy to settle to it out here. Too many distractions. I think that after all I'll go home. I've collected what I need for the first half-dozen articles. That will keep me going for a while, because preparations for the T.V. series begin next month.'

'Lord yes, it's July already, isn't it? Simon, I don't know why we're all sitting here without

207

glasses in our hands. See to it, will you? I've ordered champagne again for dinner.'

'Again?' Velma queried. 'You mean we missed out on some?'

'We had it last night, certainly. That was solely on Simon and Caroline's behalf. This evening I'm joining in with my own celebration. It's a wonderful feeling when a novel is completed, especially one which has dragged on as long as this one has. Imagine— I'll be able to read other people's books without feeling guilty!'

'For a month or two,' Giles conceded. 'Then you'll start to get restless again.'

'True, but I'll enjoy it while it lasts. Thank you, dear.' As Simon handed her a glass of sherry, 'A toast, then. Good luck, good health, and happiness. I think we can all include ourselves in that.'

They raised their glasses and again Caroline's eyes briefly met Giles's. No reaction, she thought, but what did she expect? And actually, though it was probably coincidence, there was a small nerve jumping in his cheek.

'Ruth Sinclair's expecting a baby, Grandmother,' Velma announced. 'We were talking about it before you came down.'

'I'm very happy for her.'

They spoke for a while about the Sinclairs; David's promotion, their villa, their home in Surrey. Caroline sat quietly next to Simon. She had the disturbing feeling that all this was a prelude, a marking-time, until something important happened. But what could be more important than her own engagement?

They went through for dinner and the champagne was duly poured.

'My book is finished, Gaston,' Adeline told the man-servant.

'Mes félicitations, madame.' If he wondered what the previous evening's champagne had celebrated, he was too well trained to enquire.

Velma said suddenly, 'For a newly engaged couple, you two are very subdued! I'd be dancing on the table!'

'They're overawed by the solemnity of the occasion,' her grandmother replied.

'I should have thought the solemn bit came later. When are you thinking of getting married?'

'We haven't really discussed it,' Simon answered evasively. 'In a year or so, I imagine. I'd like to get established in my new job first. Also, I doubt if Grandmother would thank me for snatching Caroline away!'

'Does she necessarily have to be snatched?' Adeline enquired. 'She'll want something to occupy her mind while you're out all day. None of that *Kinde, Kirche, Küche* nonsense, my boy!'

'Perhaps,' suggested Giles, 'she'll turn into a social butterfly and spend all her time going to coffee mornings and fashion shows.'

'I doubt it. What do you think, Caroline? Will you want to go on working?'

'It's rather early to say. As Simon told you, we haven't discussed any details yet.'

Cheese. Fruit. Coffee. This time next week she'd be—where? At the flat? At the Betts' house with Simon? Anything would be preferable to this. Her whole world seemed to have shrunk to the size of this dining-table, with Giles's eyes boring into her and Simon almost silent at her side. It had played a large part in her life, this dining-table. Across it, that first evening, Giles had learned of her disapproval of him. Here she had chatted to Marguerite Collière about Henri Duval, which had led to her meeting with him and its stormy aftermath. Amy Varley had sat here gazing at Simon with her large, hopeless eyes, and now they were drinking champagne round it to celebrate their engagement.

Caroline started violently as a tap sounded on the glass doors leading to the terrace, and, turning, she saw Paul Grant's smiling face outside. Simon went to pull back the doors and Paul and Felicity came in.

'Hi, everyone! How're things?' He bent to kiss Adeline and his eye fell on the champagne glasses. 'Say, what have we been missing?'

'I finished my novel today, Paul. Pull up a chair and join us in drinking to its success. Giles, find a seat for Felicity, will you, and Simon, some extra glasses. Would you like any fruit or cheese?'

'No, thanks. Champagne we won't refuse, but for the rest we're full up to the gills with *bouillabaisse*, if you'll forgive the not inappropriate metaphor! You're pleased with this one, Adeline? Might there be anything in it for us?'

He turned smilingly to Caroline. 'We've been wanting for some time to do a play round one of her books, but we've not managed it yet.'

'It would make a good play,' she said consideringly. 'It has a strong plot and plenty of dialogue.'

'Ah! We have an ally in the camp! Splendid!' He lifted the glass which had hurriedly been brought and filled. 'Here's to your most fantastic success yet! And may a bit of it rub off on us!'

Caroline was as grateful for the Grants' arrival as she had been on Monday for the Parkes', and for the same reason. It dispelled the intimacy of a smaller gathering. Talk became more general and her own insurmountable quietness was less noticeable.

They went into the salon and more coffee was brought. Simon put a record on the hi-fi and Velma settled next to Felicity, talking about mutual friends. Caroline hesitated. No one would notice if she slipped away for a while. Only to draw her breath, she assured herself. She wouldn't be more than ten

211

minutes. But if Giles left before she returned, so much the better.

She started across the hall, but Yvette Perrier was coming down the stairs with a vase of flowers from Adeline's room, which was removed every evening. There was no reason why Caroline shouldn't pass her, but her brain was not working clearly and at the sight of an impediment in her way, she veered instead in the direction of the study.

The shutters had not been closed and the room was lit by a pale blueness. Caroline walked over and switched on the desk lamp, standing looking down at the huddled shapes of typewriter, telephone and cassette recorder: all articles which were familiar by day but at night seemed strangely different, even faintly hostile. Would she come back to the Villa Mimosa next summer, when, perhaps, she and Simon were married? And if she did, would Giles be at Le Sirocco?

Across the room the door opened and shut quietly. Caroline's head jerked up, eyes straining to the shadows beyond the pool of light where she stood, though she already knew who it must be. Her heart began a suicidal crashing against her ribs, so painful she could hardly breathe.

Giles came slowly forward into the light.

'I suppose I should wish you happiness.'

'And don't you?' She didn't dare risk meeting his eyes in case he read too much

212

in hers.

'Against my better judgment. You don't deserve it.' His voice hardened. 'I was right all along, wasn't I? Simon's money is all that interests you.'

She made a movement of protest, but he brushed it aside. 'You were content to play him along all summer while he trailed hopefully after you and you flirted with whoever took your fancy—Tom Fawcett, Duval. But then Amy Varley loomed uncomfortably close and you felt threatened. It would have been too bad if after all the groundwork you'd put in, she snapped him up under your nose. So you decided to move in for the kill.'

The coldness which had started in the pit of her stomach was spreading like a creeping disease all over her.

'Have you finished?' Her voice was remarkably steady.

'Almost. Will you at least admit I'm right?'

'Of course you're not right.' Not quite so steady this time. She paused, tried harder. 'It has nothing to do with money.'

He gave a harsh laugh. 'I hope you're not trying to tell me you love him?'

The breath twisted in her throat. 'What right have you—'

'A certain right, as a friend of the family. Let's come down to basics. You're capable of considerable passion, Caroline, and with the best will in the world, no one could say that of

213

Simon. Have you thought about that aspect? It's not as though you won't know what you're missing.'

She said in a choked voice, 'You make it sound so—'

'Or perhaps you've never considered it as a long-term investment? Just a couple of years or so, to become established in his circle, then a handsome alimony, tiding you over till a more interesting fish comes along. I might be able to save you some trouble. Pound for pound, I imagine there's little to choose between Simon and myself, and at least there'd be no hang-ups on the physical side, would there?'

She gave a low cry and turned away distractedly, but he caught hold of her upper arm, his fingers bruising her flesh.

'How about it, Caroline? Presumably you go to the highest bidder? Marry me instead—you won't be out of pocket. Or do you need to see my bank balance before committing yourself?'

She lashed out blindly with her free hand, but he caught that too.

'Well? We have the measure of each other and at least this way no one would get hurt.'

She said in a series of gasps, 'What have I done to make you hate me so much?'

He didn't seem to have heard her. The nerve was jumping in his cheek again and his hands had begun to move up her arms to her shoulders. 'Your skin's like satin,' he said

214

jerkily. 'Is it the same all over? Shall we find out?'

He pulled her convulsively forward, mouth savaging hers, body thrusting against her. Caroline fought him desperately, choking for breath, and his lips moved to her throat.

'Perhaps you'd forgotten what we can do to each other. Do you still want to marry Simon? Do you?' His hands were moving insatiably over her, pressing, stroking, closing possessively on her breast. She felt savaged, violated, yet she ached for more. No wonder he thought so little of her; he must imagine she responded to all men this way. Knowing that her desire matched his, he was ruthless in using it against her. Somehow she had to gather the last shreds of her self-respect about her. Feebly she pushed against him, and to her surprise he let her go.

'All right.' The breath was tearing at her lungs and she had to force each word out individually. 'You've proved that you're stronger than I am. Are you satisfied? You've proved that you can hurt and humiliate me almost beyond bearing. If that's what you set out to do, you succeeded. As to why I'm going to marry Simon. I'll tell you. It's because he's the exact opposite of you. He's gentle and tender and kind. He would never deliberately hurt anyone. And if he doesn't make me feel the way you do, then I'm *glad*!' She paused, drawing more air into her tortured lungs. 'Do you hear me? *Glad!* Because to be reminded of you, ever, is the very last thing I want. There. Does that answer your question?'

She was leaning on the desk for support. 'Perhaps you'd go,' she finished dully.

Giles lifted a hand and let it fall again. In the stillness the insistent ticking of the clock took on the menace of a time-bomb. He said numbly, 'Caroline—'

And like an echo, out in the hall, came Simon's voice. 'Caro? Where are you?' And a moment later he stood in the doorway, the light of the hall behind him.

'What the hell's going on?'

Giles turned on his heel and strode past him as he came quickly into the room. 'Caro? Good grief, what's happened? Darling, are you all right?'

She said, 'Hold me, Simon.'

He reached out for her, holding her closely but gently for long minutes as she waited for a measure of calm to return to her. Then he said tentatively, 'What was all that about?'

'Just Giles being Giles.'

'Did he hurt you?'

'Yes, but it doesn't matter.'

'Of course it matters! Caro—'

'Please, Simon, I just want to forget it.'

Helplessly, not knowing how to comfort her, he went on stroking her hair. Over his shoulder she saw Adeline appear in the open doorway, hesitate, and then go quietly away

216

again. She was aching and bruised, inside and out. It might have been worth it, she thought wearily, if it had stopped her loving him, but it hadn't. He despised her as a gold-digger, taunted her with the desires he alone aroused, and all she could do was go on loving him. It was like one of the tortures of the damned.

'I think I'll go upstairs now.'

'Would you like me to send Berthe or Yvette to help you?'

'No, I'll be all right.'

His hands slipped to her arms and she winced involuntarily. The flesh was already discolouring into ugly bruises and he swore under his breath.

'He did that to you? Caro, you can't let him get away with it. Let me—'

'Forget it, Simon. Please.' She swayed and he caught her, round the waist this time.

Come along, sweetheart. Bed's the place for you.' He led her slowly up the stairs and at her bedroom door kissed her, infinitely gently. 'You're quite sure you'll be all right?'

She nodded, smiling a little to reassure him, and he opened the door for her.

The act of undressing required great concentration and she involuntarily turned her eyes from the red marks on arms and breast. She washed, brushed her hair. Now what? For a moment she stood in the centre of the room, looking vaguely round it wondered if there was anything else she ought to do. Then she lay

217

down carefully on the bed and prepared to wait for morning.

CHAPTER TWELVE

She was still lying there at nine-thirty when there was a tap on the door and Adeline Stevens came in. She went over to the girl and stood looking down on her. Caroline's lip was cut and there were livid bruises on her throat and arms. Beneath her tan her face was pale, eyes large and vulnerable.

'Oh, Caroline, my dear child!' The older woman sat down on the bed and took one of her hands. 'I'm so very sorry.'

Caroline said dully, 'I don't know what to do.'

'Do you still think Giles doesn't love you?'

'I know he doesn't.'

'And you?'

She turned her head aside and closed her eyes. After a moment Adeline said gently, 'What about Simon? You can't exorcise one man by marrying another.'

'I think we both knew it wouldn't have worked. It'll probably be a relief to him.'

'Don't think too harshly of him, child. He is extremely fond of you, but you must see how you've changed over the last months. He's not a strong character and he needs someone

218

who's weaker than himself, to give him the illusion of strength. A girl such as you've become, independent, with a spark about her, has the effect of frightening him back into his shell. Can you see that?'

'Yes. I think I always suspected it.'

Adeline patted her hand and stood up. 'Perhaps you'd better spend the day in bed. You look exhausted.'

Caroline's mouth twitched into a smile. 'Isn't it a little out of date to retire with the vapours?'

Adeline gave a bark of laughter. 'If you've managed to retain your sense of humour, you'll survive!'

There was a song, once, 'Laughing on the outside, crying on the inside'. Caroline could remember her mother singing it, but there was no point in disillusioning Adeline.

'Will you stay there? There's no need for you to come down.'

'I have to see Simon.'

'I'll send him up if you like. He's worried about you.'

'Yes, please, I think I should get it over. Then perhaps if you don't mind I will rest for a while. I didn't sleep last night.'

'Just as you like, my dear.'

Caroline's eyes closed again and she didn't see her go, but moments later Simon came quietly in and sat where his grandmother had been. His face was full of concern for her. She

219

reached for his hand and held on to it, feeling as though she were about to cast herself off from her lifeline. But in all fairness there was nothing else she could do.

'Simon —' She choked to a halt. Not a very auspicious beginning.

He said softly, 'You don't want to marry me after all, do you?'

'My feelings haven't changed, I just interpreted them wrongly. And I'm not at all sure you want to marry me, either.'

He smiled a little. 'Let's say I'm not as sure as I was of making a go of it. Quite honestly, though, Caro, I'm not the one for you. In many ways I wish I was, but you need more than I can give you. I don't exactly make you see *la vie en rose*, do I?'

She bit her lip and tasted blood as the cut opened. Simon saw it and his eyes darkened. 'Giles didn't hit you, did he?'

'Not quite.'

'Oh.' He flushed and looked away. 'I didn't realise—I thought you didn't like each other?'

'We don't,' she said tightly.

'Then how—'

'It doesn't matter.' Her voice was empty of expression and her eyes moved back to his. 'I haven't hurt you, have I? Not too much?'

'Not too much. We must have broken the record for the world's shortest engagement!'

'It was lucky your grandmother wouldn't let us tell anyone. At least there's no explaining

220

to do.'

He stood up. 'I'd better let you get some rest.'

'Yes. I'll be down later, some time this afternoon. And Simon, thank you for being so sweet about it all.'

He bent and kissed her forehead. 'See you later.'

The door closed behind him and instantly, surprisingly, Caroline fell without preamble into a deep sleep. At lunch time Adeline looked in but went away again without disturbing her. It was four o'clock before, coming slowly up from a great depth, Caroline opened her eyes again.

So her brief engagement was over, and with the minimum of heartache on both sides. Simon must realise he would have been hard pressed to control the volatile creature she had so unexpectedly become. And in due course no doubt Amy would move into her place.

About Giles, she was careful not to think at all.

For the rest of that day Caroline was limp and drained. Velma looked at her curiously when she went downstairs, but made no comment. Make-up concealed the marks on her throat and the sleeved dress her other bruises. She went back to bed straight after dinner and slept well, and by the Friday her natural resilience had reasserted itself. She spent most of the day typing out the final chapter of the novel, and by late afternoon had finished it.

That evening Simon took her out to one of the nearby restaurants for dinner. Their relationship had reverted to the affectionate, almost platonic one it had been during most of their stay at the villa. It was comforting to know that her error of judgement hadn't destroyed their basic friendship.

'You'll be coming to the party tomorrow, won't you?' he asked as they sat in the candlelight drinking coffee.

'I'd forgotten all about it.'

'There won't be any ordeal in facing people, because nobody knew about the engagement anyway.'

'Except Giles,' she said quietly.

Simon glanced up at her, then away. 'Yes. Come to think of it, he probably doesn't know it's over. Hardly surprisingly, he hasn't been back, but what *is* surprising is that Velma doesn't seem to have made any attempt to see him. She's just been lying around the pool for the last couple of days.'

'She knows she'll be seeing him tomorrow.'

'He *was* going, certainly, though I don't know—'

'Oh, he won't let a little thing like that stand in his way.' Caroline was ashamed of the bitterness in her voice.

He put a hand over hers. 'Don't let him think you're afraid of seeing him.'

'But I am,' she said simply, and knew it was the truth.

Simon sighed. 'Well, if you really don't want to go, fair enough. If you like I'll stay home and keep you company.'

'Bless you, but I wouldn't hear of it. Let's just see how I feel tomorrow. I might change my mind.'

But she knew that she wouldn't, and so did he.

There was a lack of purpose about life now that the book was finished. Caroline had nothing to do all day and found that she was bored. She was more than ready to go home. As she had hoped, her time in France had soothed away the excessive pain of her father's death, but it had produced a new one to take its place. She wouldn't be returning to London any happier than when she left.

She was in the salon with a paperback when the rest of them came downstairs ready for the party. Velma was in the lilac dress she had worn for the housewarming.

Adeline said worriedly, 'I don't like leaving you alone like this. There's still time for you to come with us.'

'Really, I'll be all right. I've an interesting book and I'm quite happy. Have a lovely time and please make my apologies to Mr Tait.'

'I'd be glad to stay with you, if you'd like me to,' Simon said again.

Caroline shook her head. 'You can tell me

223

all about it in the morning.'

But when they had gone and her straining ears could no longer hear the car engine, the house seemed very empty. Around her the large room grew dimmer. Down the steps at the dining-room end the old clock wheezed and struck ninc and beyond the pillars the hall and staircase stretched away, increasingly remote and deserted.

The kitchen door swung open suddenly, making her jump, and Berthe Perrier emerged with Caroline's supper tray. She stopped and surveyed her kindly.

'Mademoiselle looks small in this so-large room! Would you not be more comfortable in the *petit salon*?'

The study, where memories of her last meeting with Giles still clung. But it was small and cosy. It had a deep, easy chair and a door to shut out the limitless expanses of the house.

'Thank you, *madame*, I think I should.'

'I will bring the tray.'

As Caroline followed her across the hall, she wondered fleetingly what explanation Adeline had given her for Caroline's not going to the party. The woman showed no sign of curiosity. She set the tray on the now bare table which had served as a desk during the last two months.

'Would you prefer that my husband and I remain in the kitchen until the family returns?'

'No, thank you, *madame*. I shan't need

224

anything else.'

'Very well. We will be in the annexe if you want us. Goodnight, *mademoiselle*.'

Caroline ate the appetising meal slowly. She must try to remember some of Berthe's recipes to enliven her frugal meals back in London. She loved the food of Provence—olives and aubergines, peppers and garlic, *bouillabaisse*—

She reached quickly for her paperback, holding it in one hand and forcing her eyes down the pages as she finished the last of her meal. It wasn't safe to relax her guard for one moment. When her plate was empty she took it back to the kitchen and stood for a moment looking round the empty room. A plait of garlic hung from the wall, a huge glass dome covered the cheese board, and the last traces of Gaston's Gauloise hung on the air. Oh, France! When would she come again?

She went back to the study, but her concentration was broken and she couldn't settle to her book. It was very warm and the smallness of the room, which before had comforted her, now seemed claustrophobic. She opened the window, pushed back the shutters and stepped out on to the terrace. It was very quiet. An owl hooted down in the pines by the pool. Through the stillness the sound of an approaching car on the main road reached her clearly. The sound grew louder, as though the driver had turned down into Avenue Pascal, and a moment later the engine

225

cut off.

Caroline straightened, listening. Surely Simon hadn't returned to her after all? But she heard the distant click of the gate and footsteps coming quickly towards the house. He'd see the study light, because she'd left the door ajar.

She turned from the balustrade, looking back into the room at an angle in time to see the door open wider to admit Giles.

She didn't move, didn't even think, except to be grateful that her back was hard up against the reassuring solidness of the balustrade. He came in slowly and stopped in the middle of the room.

'If you tell me to go, I shall at once.'

She turned away, leaning over the balustrade, eyes staring sightlessly down into the darkness of the grass below. After a moment he came and stood beside her.

'Thank you for that, at least. It's more than I deserve.'

Silence again. Then he said, 'I'm running out of ways to apologise. I knew you wouldn't see me if I called, and any letters or flowers I sent would be thrown away out of hand. My only chance, and it was a slim one, seemed to be Jeremy's party. But you didn't come.' He paused. 'Caroline, I'm tired of fencing around. I wouldn't have come now if it hadn't been for Adeline. She's known for months that I'm so besotted with you I can't think straight. She seemed to think, God knows why, that it might be worth my telling you.'

Caroline was hardly breathing, afraid to make the slightest movement in case it shattered this fragile thing that was beginning to grow.

'Actually,' he went on, 'on the principle of having nothing to lose, I'd reached the same conclusion, though heaven knows you can't be in much doubt about my feelings.'

She said steadily, 'I know you want to go to bed with me. You made that clear enough.'

'My dearest girl, if that had been all I'd have taken a cold shower weeks ago! There's no problem finding sex when you want it, but this—total commitment is something I've never experienced before.' He leant beside her on the balustrade and she saw how tightly his hands were clenched together.

'When I found out about your father, I told myself I hadn't a hope. I even thought I'd come to terms with it, till I heard of your engagement. And you kept so close to Simon that evening, it began to look as though you might really love him. I simply couldn't take it—not without one last try. And of course I went about it the worst possible way.' He was silent for a few minutes, then he said, 'Would you believe that I've never in my life told a girl I loved her? Because it's the truth. There's never been anyone I couldn't have managed quite comfortably without. Until now. When you didn't arrive with the others tonight, it brought home to me very forcibly how unthinkable life would be without you.'

He straightened and turned towards her. 'So there you have it. I love you, Caroline, though it's time someone invented a new word, because it doesn't come anywhere near to expressing—' He drew a deep breath. 'Aren't you going to say anything at all?'

'I'm not sure that I can,' she said in a whisper, 'except that I love you, too.'

He reached for her and she went swiftly into his arms, feeling the thunderous, beating of his heart against hers. He said, 'I'm not sure that I believe this. It didn't seem remotely possible.'

She drew his head down to hers, feeling the tremor go through him as his arms tightened round her. But although the remembered currents flowed powerfully between them, this kiss was different from those that had gone before. Caroline was conscious for the first time of his holding back, considering her rather than himself even when she would have preferred him not to. He was right, though, she thought wonderingly, as his hands moved with a new, almost reverent tenderness, over her back and shoulders. They could afford to hold back now, because there was no longer the need to test each other, no desperation or anger or resentment, just a depth of loving they were only on the fringes of discovering, and which they could explore together for the rest of their lives.

She said dreamily, 'Do you realise we're standing almost exactly where we were the first time you kissed me?'

Giles brushed his lips over hers. 'That was incredible, wasn't it—spontaneous combustion! It just about knocked me sideways but I wouldn't admit it. Having kept my cool very satisfactorily for the last twenty years or so, I strongly resented the position I found myself in. Even so, I couldn't keep away from you, and the fact that you obviously loathed the sight of me didn't help at all.'

She heard the smile come into his voice. 'I thought perhaps it might get you out of my system if I made love to you!'

'And would it have done?' She was glad the semi-darkness hid her heightened colour.

'You didn't give me the chance to find out!' He laughed softly. 'No, darling, of course it wouldn't, because for the first time in my life it wasn't a purely physical thing. And oddly enough, though I wanted to like hell, there was a certain—relief, almost, every time you drew back. Don't ask me why. It was as though, if you hadn't, something would have been spoiled.' He gave a short, embarrassed laugh. 'And that, coming from me, is the most blatant hypocrisy!'

He put his hand under her chin and gently raised her head. 'Darling, I have to ask this. Why did you agree to marry Simon?'

'Because I was sure you didn't love me, and I couldn't have borne to go through it all again. It seemed safer to settle for affection and companionship.' She met his eyes. 'You didn't really think it was his money, did you?'

'No, but I tried to. It was preferable to believing you really loved him.' His voice sobered. 'When I saw him tonight, I thought he was going to hit me. Presumably it was because of the other evening, and I can't blame him. How do you think he'll take this?'

'I doubt if it'll come as much of a surprise. And he didn't really want to marry me any more, it was just that he was too sweet to back out of it.' She laid her cheek against his. 'The trouble was that you didn't give me enough time, on the beach, to take in what you'd said about Daddy, and when Simon and Velma came I didn't have the chance. I tried to tell you on the boat—'

'I realise that now, but at the time it all seemed hopeless, which was why I took refuge in poor Velma.'

'Giles—'

'Sweetheart, that was over, such as it was, by the end of last summer. I didn't see her at all in London. Possibly she might have thought we'd take up again, but I met you the first evening, and that was more or less that. I think she suspected pretty early on, and after that ghastly day on the boat she asked me outright how I felt about you. I hedged, of course, but

I'm sure she knew. She was a little piqued, but certainly not hurt.'

They were silent for a while, holding each other close and going over in their minds all the mistakes and misunderstandings that had finally brought them to this moment.

Caroline said softly, 'If only Daddy could have been here, to wish us well!'

'Yes. You know, in the hospitality suite before the programme, he suddenly said, "I wish you could meet my daughter." I don't know what made him say it, and someone else came up then, so I couldn't ask him. But considering everything that's happened, it was rather odd, wasn't it?'

Her mouth trembled. 'Then I think we can take it we have his blessing.' And as Giles bent his head again to hers, she felt there was nothing in the world to cloud her happiness.